The Silence Between Us

Jamie Smyth

Contents

Chapter 1

Greetings,I'm Adhya, 23 years old and the only child in my family. I reside with my father, whom I fondly call Paapa, and my mother, lovingly referred to as Amma. We belong to an upper-middle-class background and call a town our home, not a bustling city.

And i'm indian modern girl. Who goes with ever kind attire, so I go with kurtas jeans crops shorts dress etc I am doing my msc in Biotechnology(final sem). I dreamed to continue my studies and do my masters but i think after i'm join the courses and college then i come to know that if you dream dream dream then something you should pay for it. Its nothing like that i'm facing some problem it just a college trauma, because i am person who enjoy every single minute.

My suffering are like i should get up early, attend college attend classes do assignment to my projects and come back and do with my college starts and sleep by late night and have become like a robert. I know education is sometimes to gain but sure i'm losing everything like like my vision, my weight, hair, even my haemoglobin level is also every low and most important thing interested studying i don't say that i am the first rank student but still live manage to get my 70%.

Good reason behind losing interest in college of studies maybe a college rules where i have done my bachelors different colleges where we use to bunk, enjoy have fun, attend cultural event even in sport's etc it was complete filmy vibe college life. And our gang was quite famous not quite famous we were famous in college so i got it to such a horrible college know. Add story behind this, once i just back answered my lecturer sorry my HOD that to by using the word FUCK and got suspended for 1 week that to it my final yest. Coming from a middle class family and getting suspended is big matter and my complete freedom was destroyer.So my parents searched good discipline boarding college too my masters. Don't get the surprised by listening that 21 your old girl going to boarding school sorry college i am i am the ones who attended sorry attending my college has a border with cotton kurta patiala pant and to dupatta. Yes there are colleges likes, for more detail you can contact Adhya for jail vibe college. After 3 months and going to leave bloody fucking college and then having my peaceful life again.

Don't expect too much because my routine wake up at 5am Study, break fast, go to college by 7am, attend class, do project get scolding from your guide for mistake in your project come back and get freshen up do your homework studying sleep repeat repeat repeat repat. Fuck fuck fuck.

After 3 months.

After coming from my college. I decided to take 3 months break before starting my career so i have turned into introvert by ending that sach kind of colleges, I need some break to see myself and come back to my normal life.

All my friends are working or doing there studies in abroad so i left alone in my hometown so have decided something to do for myself so and this time being i have started reading books i am not that good reader and I take atleast 1 year to complete a book but still i am managing to read quite fast and my favorite is gardening.

We have a good new tenant whoever recently moved in 6 months. They are sweet and comfortable. And they have son who is 2 year younger than me. But he have become a good friend within few days and no much about what there family but i know that uncle aunty and he is Advish and he have one more elder brother who is a intern surgeon. Advish and I share common education stream but never ever we have discuss about it. Where his parents are government offical so they have relocated here. Though all my friends are busy he is the one who accompany me ever time actually vise versa because even he is new to this town so i'm helping him to explore.

Am a single child but my parents never showed that single child missing live or maybe they are hiding it, they are strict towards my education and life style by behavior. But they are loving caring and give my privacy a typical asian parents.

I now I have caused some many problem to my parents. So many complaints in school and college, the damage I have done, my fight with my neighbor and schoolmates etc etc. Yes i'm a trouble maker to my parents.

After I join my college in that boarding college, they have seen changes in me so there planning to send me for work in the city. Yes I liked to independent but I still enjoying being lazy.

After completing my msc and 3 months of vacation in my home, my paapa has a job for me so I should give my interview next week so I getting ready for interview. Not that I really interested but I dont want to be embarrassment so I my getting ready for it.

Chapter 2

Hey, I'm Adishh,I reside with my parents, daddy, mummy, and my brother Advish, in a new town due to my parents' recent relocated because my parents are government officials . Although I've visited once, I'm not one for conversations or making new friends-I'm an introvert.

Proudly a doctor and aspiring surgeon, I thrive in my studies, scoring 80% in my medicine degree. A punctual student, my routine involves early morning jogging, hospital rounds, OT sessions, and an evening shift from 2 to 8 pm. This peaceful routine has been my comfort for two years.

I know i'm boring for many of them still I have own comfort zome. Not to appreciate or phrase my self I was quite famous in my college days and even in hospital reason I every obedient and okay I said that I am good looking guy in colleges. I'm my hospital I have a name junior golden hand because my guide is golden hand because he never failed in any operation. I have studied hard only to join under him.

I have call session with my parents everyday in 9pm, when ever they call I come across one name adhya that to my brother every 10min will be her topic. She is interesting but dead opposite to my character. Can imagine how is she maybe good looking, fun loving, enjoying and talkative.

Where i'm I only have 2 friends one is Jeevan my childhood friend and Trishul my colleague come good friend in hospital. And my guide from my hospital my senior doctor Dr.Rajesh. Dr.Rajesh is super cool doctor in my lifetime I'll never ever find a doctor like him who is cool supportive.

One good morning I got a call from my father telling is there my vacancy in my hospital for a biotechnology graduate. It was for Adhya. So inform about this to my senior doctor and I made a call and alloted a interview for her. It was super fast than I expected. I just informed about this to my daddy.

Chapter 3

Adhya pov:

It was my interview day I have no expectations about my new job. Because it was a super multi-speciality hospital and a number one hospital in the city of bangalore yes it is in Bangalore. And most of the doctor are foreign return. Now you can imagine I never have so much expectation that I will get job in this hospital.

I'm infront of the hospital which was huge and looked like expensive hospital. My confidence level was dropping and warm hand embrace my shoulder it gave me some confidence it was my paapa and we walked in. Paapa made a call for someone with no time a good looking, formal dressed man arrived he introduced him self has Trishul. "Sorry uncle he have OT to attend, so I will be guiding you know" he said and we both nodded our head. After taking lift for 6th floor he took us for a lavishing board room and under level of confidence was stopped.

"uff man, what to do now, I know that I won't pass this interview atleast I should not look dumb infront of hiring team." My subconscious conversation was disturb my papa

"all the best go attend the interview"

I had never face stage fear but now my whole body was shivering. Not because I'm attend interview it was the hospital and my first attempt toward my success is going to fail it was haunting my mind.

I entered the interview area there 5 people where 4 with smiley face, one is like a solemn face who is 50s age uncle.

I greeted them with great smile.

They just smile and instructed to be seated.

"Good morning sir" I said

With in a second I got questions firing on me. I dont know how did I answer there question my not even had space to breath or to think. All I know that I was answering there questions. After 20min one of the interviewer said "wait outside for 10min".

I said same thing to paapa and trishul

Trishul asked "who was there in the interview panel".

I only remember that one face and said "Dr.Krishnan".

Without any hesitation he said "wtf, then are you 100% sure you have given your interview the best".

Before he complete the sentence I got a call to get in.

Again with those 5faces I seated in same place.

Dr.krishnan said "you will working under me has a research associated for my gastro-oncology(it is stomach and gut related cancer studies) and for first 3month I will keep you has s trainee or you can call it has a intern".

Without thinking for second I said "okay sir" with full of happy and excitement. Then my mind flashed Dr.Trishul expression and I was confused.

And he called one of the HR and he start saying about procedure about recruiting and comes my salary package and I was so curious and its 30k has a intern after 3month completing my intern period it will 50k.

Damn I never ever thought I would get my a huge salary in my initial days.

With my happy face, I felt the board room, and HR addressed me, saying wait out for 30 minutes; she will be back with paper. I nodded and thanked her, and I came out. After seeing my happy face, paapa and Dr.Trishul got an idea, and they congratulated me.

Dr.Trishul dialed someone and said, "Hey, she got a job, but under Dr. Krishnan, will you join us for lunch?"

But Dr. Krishnan was pressed and told by Dr. Trishul that made me still confusing, but to ask about it, it was too late because everything was completed, only paper work was pending.

After 30 minutes of waiting, HR came back with a paper, which I signed.

Again, Trishul made a call again, after 5 minutes, I saw a handsome doctor who is 6.2 feet tall, has a fair complexion, a perfect body, a doctor scrub (it is a doctor dress most of the surgeon wears), a knee-length white apron (doctor white coat), round specs, and ID hanging out of the pocket of the apron with two pens. He was so perfect; he was like hero material who has become a doctor. My own subconscious said, "How lucky he's girlfriend is."

I was seeing him by just adjusting my hair.

Adishh pov

When Trishul called and said that her recruiting was done, he invited me for lunch because it was lunch break. I felt happy for no reason; that feel can not be described by words. Though I was tried for 7 hours of operation, I still want to join them, and I want to see the masterpiece that Advish was explaining.

Has I been close to them, I saw a girl who was wearing simple simple red kurtas and was playing with her hair or adjusting her little tense and full of happiness. Damn, I never admired a girl like this before. When I reach, with all her hesitation, or I can see some blush she left hair open.

Oh my God I had a mini-heart attack. "Shit, what is Adhishh? Be a gentleman."

I greeted her father first, and he introduced his daughter to me and said,

"He is the one who helped you get a job here. He is the son of his neighbor, Mr. Chandrakanth."

Within a second, she said, "Advish brother, ahh. Introvert fell...o w," lowering her tone.

Her father gave her a faint look, and she just bit her soft pink lips and looked at me.

"What should I tell her? Hey, is it okay or not? I'm not like that," but all the words were buried in my mind, and I gave her a mild, simple smile.

And we planned to have lunch in our cafeteria, we get quite good good her.

She was very confused about the menu to choose; her father was comfortable with chatpati and curry. She was going through the menu and struggling to decide.

I had all the confidence and made up my mind to speak with her. I said, "Go with fried rice and panner fry it, my personal favorite."

Looking at me, she just opening her mouth, and my confidence and heart are both broken.

"Che...how boring," and by time, Trishul chuckled. I stared at him.

By now, she said, "I go with butter masala dosa and good coffee" and looked at me.

To compromise my ego, I looked at her and said, "To order this, you are struggling from the past 5 minutes."

Her father added a sentence. "Thank God it's just 5 minutes; to order the same two biriyani in a hotel, she sometimes takes 15 minutes."

She looked at me annoyingly.

By that moment, I came to know that I fucked up.

Chapter 4

After every procedure is done for Adhya's recruiting, her appointment is after 10 days."Paapa, should I join PG or?"Mr. Shekar (Adhya's father) looked at Adishh.

"Uncle, though PG is comfortable, they are a bit costly, and she should compromise with food, so it's better to rent a house."

By this time, Adishh has become trustworthy in Shekar's eyes.

"That sounds good, Adishh. Let me arrange a well-furnished home for her."

Adishh pov

I don't know why the words spill out of my mouth.

"Uncle, if you don't mind, there is a flat for rent that is just opposite my flat."And my subconscious slapped me hard.

Without any hesitation, Uncle said,"It's a very good idea."By then, Adhya and Trishul were surprised by our conversation."Paapa""No words, Adhya; I will arrange everything by 10 days."

After saying farewell to then.Trishul looked at me in a teasing way.

"What, bro, is there anything like...""Shut up, there my good neighbor."

"Then help me; I will try on her."

Those words irritated me.

"Trishul... Just get lost, Orles. I will complain about your 4 days of sick leave."

After 7 days of their meetings

Adhya pov

One fine Friday night in my home. I and Amma were busy packing my bags, though I'm leaving my home two days prior to Bangalore, just to set everything up in my new home. "I have packed all the dry masala, some ready-to-go foods, and some instant food items to share with Adishh too." Amma said to me.

"Haa haa, I will." I nodded to her.

And she gave me 10k. I was shocked.

"I know Paapa has given you enough money to spare your monthly expenses; still keep this; it will help you," she said with teary eyes.

I was touched by the words, but still, with my naughty face, I smiled at her, which brought a smile to her face too.

Early morning, at 5.30 am, Amma was waking me up with all the energy.

"Wake up, it's getting late."

"This early do I have any meet Sheelu?"(Sheela Adhya's mother).

"Today you should move to Bangalore."

All my sleep vanished in a second.

"Yes, yes, I will be ready by 30 minutes."

In Bangalore.

We are opposites of my new apartment; it was good-looking, and I was happy with my apartment.

By then, Adishh comes with casuals with simple joggers and a T-shirt; he was looking good in that too.

Our flat was on the 8th floor, and we took all our luggage.

Flat was pretty cool and cute; it was one BHK home with a fully furnished home with a cute shaded blue-colored sofa, a simple six-seated dining table, a small and sufficient kitchen, one bedroom with a king-size bed, and a balcony. It gave me confidence so quickly.

After arranging everything, Adishh ordered some food, and we had it together with my parents. They felt it by late afternoon.

At 6 in the evening the same day.I thought of renovating my room and living area. With all the stuff I have bought in the past I altered my living area and room. It was looking aesthetic, like I dreamed. It was my home with all the cute and colorful stuff.After doing all my work, I planned to invite Adishh tomorrow for a housewarming party for a good lunch. So I planned everything and went to call him.

Adishh pov.

I heard a nocking at my door by 9.30 p.m.It was Adhya; I was surprised by her entry.

"I thought of a housewarming party, so please don't miss. I will be happy if Dr.Trishul also joins us."

She handed me a bowl of sweets, and I took the sweet.

"Hey, its fine, you carry on with your friend." - Adish

"I don't have any close friends in this city; I have only you as a friend currently here. Don't miss; I have already arranged everything." - Adhya.

I was happy with her words, and I nodded with a smile.

It was a Sunday.

I am completing my morning routine and all my work because I have to attend her party.

It was already 11 a.m. when I decided to visit early. Even Trishul is going to join us.

By 11.30, I went to her home.

She greeted me with a heartwarming smile; it was blissful.

I just entered her home; it had a different vibe from yesterday's plan, and her boring house had undergone a transformation into a colorful, lively home. With all the colorful stuff on the sofa, contracting pillows, dream catchers hanging on the wall, photos and paintings all over the wall, cute dolls, and toys there and there, I never thought this boring flat could also be turned into an aesthetic home.

I heard some beautiful voices calling names...

Adhya pov.

Around 11.30 a.m., I heard a doorbell. It was Adishh with a white rose and lily mixed flower bouquet, one flower pot, and a gift bag. With a smile on his face.

"Hii. Come in."

And he handed over all the gifts he bought.

And he was looking all around my home with a surprise look.

"May I know the reason behind your surprise look, Adishh?"

"No. I was looking at your organized home; thats it; it is beautiful when you arranged all this; that too you shifted to yesterday."-Adishh

"Paapa explained about that flat, so I planned every day for the past 8 days, bought it, and here I placed it," I said with all rhythm.

He smiled in the corner of his mouth."Advish called me yesterday, and he told me to never visit anyone." I questioned him.

"That means I should go back now."And he turned around to go back.Within a second, I held his hand, nodding my head. "I was kidding."By then, there was another doorbell.I was looking towards the door to open it; it was a delivery boy.

Adishh pov

The moment she held my hand, I started shivering all over my body. It was not the first time that girls held my hands; there are multiple examples, but this time the feeling was different.

By then, the delivery boy had interrupted the moment.She collected all the delivery items.

Looking towards me, "coffee or tea"

"No trouble; I will drink when Trishul comes".

"Then come, I will take you hometour."

"Hey, it's okay. To spare my time, I will read books.".

I really wanted to go with her, but I still restricted myself.

"Hey, I won't irritate or distrub; feel free." I nodded for her words.

She followed with a 10-minute home tour. She has organized her home so well.

And she said, "Don't mind, can you help me out by arranging food?"

It was shocking for me. Never in my life was I alone at any girl home and arranging food with her.I was questioning what was wrong with me and what I was doing, but I was still comfortable with her, and I enjoyed that moment.

After arranging everything,.Trishul joined us even though he has a gift for her and a flower pot.

"Hey, I love plants. I planned to buy more now that I have two plants already.""Hey, that's nice. We can go shopping this evening." - Trishul

"Are you sure if both of you are free when we can?"

Both of them looked at me.

"Okay, fine, we can go shopping some other day; maybe he is busy. I dont want to disturb you both; you both have already spared too much time." Ahe said, With disappointment in her eye.

"Okay, but only for 2 hours; you both should be quick." I said to them.

Both hi-fied with full excitement.

We having all the lunch she has ordered, there was fried rice and panner fry.

I was shocked by her move and made me happy.

By serving fried rice and panner fry "Its boring, but still taste"- Adhya

" Thank you...."

After finishing our lunch, we decided to go for shopping.

Chapter 5

After lunch, they went shopping for new home decor.

Adhya pov

By taking Adishh's car, we went to a plant shop (nursery). There were a number of plants. So we purchased some cute indoor plants, some pots, plant seeds, a coco pit, and sand.

And the bill was around 2500 rupees; it was too much for my current budget. So I know I have only one way to bargain.With all the bargaining knowledge.

"Hey, 2500 is too much; can I find all this around 1500? So tell me the discounted and exact price."

I can see shock and an embarrassing look in both Adishh and Trishul.

"Ma'am, 1500 will be every low price, so with all discounts, it will be 2200."- shopkeeper

"No, 2200. The last price I will pay is 1750, or else I don't want this."

By this dialogue, both are ready to leave the shop.

"Okay, then add 150 more, so pay around 1900," said the shop-keeper.

"Fine, I will pay 1850; this is final; I can't give more," so I placed the exact amount on the table.

By this time, the shopkeeper has handed over all the purchased items.

"You have very good bargaining skills, ah." - Trishul

"Of course, a woman is always a woman; all this comes from her blood."

All three of us laughed and sat in the car.

"You gave us 2 hours of time, but still there is 1 hour and 5 minutes left so we can explore the market," I questioned Adishh.

"Okay"- Adishh

Adishh pov.

I was mesmerized by her bargaining skills; damn, she saved around 600 rupees. If I were there in her place, I would have paid the full amount.

When she asked about exploring markets, I was happy because I would get some more time to spend with her. She made me explore myself in my own way. I was comforted, enjoying, and cherishing her company with all my heart and soul.

We were at a local market. It was a huge market place where you could find everything but was crowded.

"You know, exploring a local market is the best idea." - Adhya

"I have been to the market but never felt that it was a spot to explore something," I said with a pale face. Because it was not a comfortable place for me.

"Bro, life is all to learn; today's lesson is to learn how to explore markets and how to bargain," Trishul said with laughter.

"So funny," Adhya.

The first zone of the market is the flower market.

We were in a flower market, with all types of flowers all aroun d.First, I went near a Jasmine, selling Aunty, and looked around at all the different kinds of jasmine. And select one.

The surprising part was that by then, after purchasing jasmine flowers, she had a very good conversation, and she introduced us both (Trishul and Adishh) to her.

"Aunty, these both are doctors, so you can ask or tell about your health issue if you have."

She taps her head.

I just gave her money for the jasmine she bought before.

"Is he his husband or boyfriend?" By saying this, she looked at Adhya.

Before I correct her,

"He is my friend, Aunty, not more than that." - Adhya.

The next 15 minutes were spent on a photo session; I had never considered taking a photo or selfie in a crowded market before. These two monkeys were out of their control; they had multiple video photos and selfies with me too. But my heart literally didn't want to stop her.But her joy around the market was blissful; never in my life would I enjoy so much in the market.Her laughter, enjoyment, cuteness, and naughty acts around the market made me lost in her world.

Now comes the food zone.

There was a pani puri stall, and looking at that, Adhya pointed her finger towards it.

"Hey, I don't like pani puri," said Trishul.

"Are you belong to man-kind species," Adhya.

Trishul stared at her.She changed her sight direction and looked at me.

"I eat pani puri, but I won't call it my personal favorite." I said to miss her taunting dialogue.

"Okay, then give a company to eat." - Adhya.

She explained how the pani puri should be to the vendor, and he gave us two plates of pani puri.

I should not lie, it was the best pani puri in my life, and one more best moment was she. The way she enjoyed her plate of food was beauteous.

After pani puri, a plate of momos, cotton candy, and ending with ice cream.

Uff, she finally completed her market tour.

By then, it was 8 p.m. Our market tour was completed in 3 hours.

"You said to spare 1 hour, 5 minutes; see, you know it's around 3 hours in the market." - Adishh.

"Sorry," she pouted. "Leave him; he is always like this, but it was so memorial to me. I enjoyed it a lot, despite all my work tension. Thank you for everything, but I should leave. Don't mind." - Trishul.

And then both of them are hugged side by side and trishul left by greeting me. Now I and Adhya are the only two left.

Yes, I'm a bit comfortable with her, but still, in the back of my mind, there is some hesitation. I can't expect her to start a conversation every time.

It was a 45-minute journey from the market to our apartment.

Well, driving the car, I had a doubt. Sorry, conformation.

"When we first met, you said that I am an introvert. How can you come to the conclusion that I am an introvert when you see me for the first time in your life?" It sounds rude, but I wanted a conclusion for that.

I was expecting embarrassment in the her but still, there was a little smile, and she said,

"I don't think you are an introvert. I hope you never met the right person or comfort zone of person in your life. Yes, I am sorry all this happened because, according to your brother Advish, he told me that you never ever open up with anybody in your life, your silent, you never going to talk with anybody that east,you take time to get open up with some, you never love fun. This is the description that your brother gave me. So i come to the conclusion that your a introvert, of course introvert live like this but you look different talk to me nicely comfort zone with me with no time you." It was an express train with no stops.

I suddenly put up a break to my car by listening to one nonstop word.And her words, YOUR NOT INTROVERT, made my heart sedative. Yes, I need this kind of tranquilizing in my life. I felt that I had been waiting for this moment for decades; I wanted to leave those moments. She made me so cozy that moment, or maybe my entire life. My heart was saying you are in love, but my mind was saying that is just attraction.

"Hey, what happened? Why did you stop the car?" - Adhya.

Coming out of all my thoughts: "Just repeat what you said now."

"Y-O--U-R N-O-T I-N-T-R-O-V-E-R-T" She pressed each word and said, I don't know how she came to know that I was expecting the same thing from her mouth.

My heart says, "Bro, she is just what you need."

My mind says, "Bro, I think practically only two sentences aren't enough to leave my entire life with her."

"Hello, Mr. Doctor, do you need any special invitations to start your car?" Adhya said with a childish accent.

"No, no, I was about to," said Adishh.

"I have a deal for you. I think I should take an everyday cab or auto from flat to the hospital, so let's make a deal. You can pick me up and drop me off when you're free. I can pay for it."

"Fine, no need pay, I can pick you up and drop you off, but I can't assure you that all the time will be convenient for you because I have different schedules and operations all over."

"Okay, whenever you are free, you can text, so we can go together. Take my number," she said, taking my phone, which escaped in the dashboard, and "What's the password?"

I don't know what flashed in her mind, and she just passed my phone to my hand, but without taking the phone, I said password "337650."

"Go slow, bro. I am not that intelligent like you to remember all your mystery numbers in one second."

"It's not a mystry number; it's my admission number for my MBBS. Last 6 digits: 337 650." Now I said it very slowly.

She just dialed the number and saved it.By then, we reached the apartment, and she gave me a little pot of cactus.

"Good night, Adishh. See you tomorrow. Please don't call before 8; it's my sleeping time. You're going early, just drop a message, let's say bye," and she ran inside the flat.

I chuckled at her act and words.

All my thoughts were engrossed by Adhya, so my sleep was gone the only flim running in mind was Adhya.

Chapter 6

A dhya pov

It was the first day of work, so I decided to keep my attire simple, so I went with a simple peach-colored kurta and white leggings. Not to wear a dupatta because I used to carry my white coat or apron all over the hospital.

At 7.30am, I got a text from Adishh saying, "I will be leaving at 8.15am."

However, my shift was also from 8.30 a.m. to 5 p.m. I was also convenient with times.

So I got ready, finished my pooja, had my breakfast, and left my flat at 8.15 a.m.Both of us work for a hospital, so it is mandatory for both of us to wear formal attire. So he was in a black pant and white formal shirt with formal shoes. Stethoscope and apron in hand.

We left and reached the hospital.

Adishh pov

Once she left,

I went for out patient's rounding; one of my colleagues was on leave, so I had to cover that sift.

So my schedule was busy, so I texted Adhya, "Before you leave, just text me. If I am free, I will drop you."

Even my afternoon schedule was busy. So I didn't get time to meet her. Even I did not text or call her. Even I didn't text her.

After all my sift was over, I was about to leave. Just for confirmation, I called her. "Where are you? I was about to leave."

"5 minutes" and she hangs up the call.

A dull, lifeless face of Adhya was walking towards me. It is pinching my heart.

Without saying a word, she sat in the car. The whole time we traveled in our car, we both maintained silence.

I was expecting her to tell me all about her first-day experience, but her silence was discouraging.

By then we reached our apartment, and even in the lift, she continued her silence. I was losing all my patience. Before she could open her door lock, I pulled her into my flat. I made her sit and gave her some water. She drank a full glass of water and looked at me.

"What happened?" -Adishh

She wrapped her hand around my waist and started crying so hard and gripping the hug tight again and again.

"What happened, Adhya? If you cry like that, I'll get tensed."

Breaking her hug "I don't want this job, Adi (Adishh). I can't continue this job. Nobody talks to me, nobody cares about my presence, and I have nobody in the department to speak to; at least there is no one in my age group. All are busy with their work; even on my first day of work, I had loads of work, but still there is work pending." She said this while crying hiccups.

I was gloomy about her situation.

"I can understand your situation, Adhya; everyone faces this. In the initial days, work will be hectic; after that, it will come back to normal."

"It's not about the hectic workload, Adi. I dreamed of a good workspace environment. I can't go again. Even there, nobody was my good friend circle. I was lost in all my original behavior. I feel the same here. I'm going end up like a robot who eats, works, and sleeps."

"I will feel alone in the hospital; I will leave Adi all alone."By this time, she was starting to sob her heart out.

Her tears, her swollen eyes, her reddish cheeks, and the pressure she is going through made me insane; it was hurting me too.

I kneel down to her face level, cupping her face.

"You have Adishh, Adhya." -Adishh

She gave a surprise look with the same teary face.

"I mean, in the hospital, you have me; even Trishul will be with you."

"Sorry, we both were busy."

She started to wipe away all her tears and looked at me.

"Promise" and showed our little fingers towards me.

What?" said Adishh.

"Pinky promise"-Adhya.

And she told me the steps to make her kind of promise.

"Thank you," Adhya

She was about to leave. I just held her hand and said, "Let's have dinner together. I will order something."

"Okay"- Adhya

"What you want to have"-Adishh.

"Double spicy ramen and chocolate ice""Are you crazy who will eat those spicy noodles?"- Adishh.

"I will; only food can fix my mood.".

"Okay with spicy ramen, but not a double spicy one."- Adish

"Okay, fine, doctor," Adhya said, nodding her head.

After 30 minutes, our order was delivered.Her spicy ramen, ice cream, and my Italian egg omelet and vegetable salad-by then I had prepared some fresh apple juice for both.

We started digging for food.After one bite of her ramen, she slowed her blow to take a bit.

"I'm not that comfortable with chopsticks."- Adish

"Okay, then take it," she said, placing her chopsticks with some noodles near my mouth.

"Oh sorry,..."

I just took some noodles and filled my mouth.

"Do you have a girlfriend?" She questioned me suddenly.

I chucked and started coughing with all the food inside my mouth, and I managed to swallow it.And gave her a surprise look.

She will put a glass of water in her"Eat slowing; I just asked; I did not interrogate you."

"No. I was surprised by your question."- Adishh.

"I just thought of asking, that's it."

"I don't have any; do you want to take a chance?" I flirted with her.

She blushed. And I was shocked."Oh, sorry, you're not my type."

"Wtf,"

"Okay, okay, I will be your girlfriend. Will you marry me?" she showed her hand, meaning to put a ring, and laughed.Her move made me shiver in my spine.

"Okay, okay, let's finish the food. I have still more to complete."

We both finished our food, and she helped with cleaning.

"Okay, bye, good night. You have kept your flat very boring; I will help you renovate it. Okay, bye."

I stepped towards her and hugged her tightly. "I know what you're facing, but remember, you have Adishh by your side; don't cry; everything will be."

She slowly moved her hand and wrapped around me. "Will you?"

"Picky promise"

And I break a hug, and I hold her shoulder. "Good night, have a peaceful sleep.".And she left.

It was only 3 days before we both started to speak to each other. But she was completely out of my comfort zone. To what extent is it comfortable to flirt with her, hug her, and console her.

Adhya pov.

I know that I exaggerated the situation, but people have high expectations and dreams, and when things come in different shades, they will break down.If Adishh hadn't questioned me or cared about my silence, I would have stayed strong, calmed my inner self, and been back to normal after a good sleep. You may think your strong comfort arm around you will make you melt out of your emotions.

He's hug, he's words, he's consolement made my mind relief; it was warm, it was special, it was heartful.He had already made a special place in my life. But I can't name our relationship. Maybe it will be fast if I give a relationship tag.I was trying hard to fit into my workspace. It is more hectic than that; I'm alone. In the hospital premises, I will get Trishul or Adishh, both of whom would accompany me most of the time, but in my workspace, I'm the only one in my 20s; all are above 30 and most are in their 50s.

It has been one week since I joined the job.

My friendship with Trishul is as follows: we both fight, taunt each other, gossip about each other, and make stupid things around us. We both have built a good bond.

Where Adishh and I are pretty close, I start and end by only telling him all my stupid stories. He cares for me, tolerates me, and supports me in everything.

When we three are together, the vibe is different, and we all enjoy it. I and Trishul make idiotic work, where Adishh slows his maturity and solves it. It's like a mother taking care of two children.

Chapter 7

It has been 3 months and i have completed my internship paid by then i am very comfortable and say very comfortable but all is going good with my job. I used to spend the most of the time but Adishh and trishul, it was fun going in hospital.

As the days unfold, I find myself falling even deeper for Adishh. The bond we share goes beyond being merely good; it's becoming an enchanting connection that warms my heart. Every moment spent in his company feels like a cherished chapter, and I've grown to savor not just his presence but the comforting warmth he effortlessly brings into my life.

His caring gestures, whether intentional or not, act as a magnetic force, pulling me closer to him with each passing day. In the midst of this growing affection, I can't help but wonder about the nature of his feelings. Is he sensing the same magnetic pull, considering us as close friends, or am I simply a part of his responsibilities?

Despite the uncertainty, these three months have left an indelible mark on my heart. I am undeniably smitten by Adishh, and the journey of falling for him is unfolding like a beautiful story, one that I'm eager to explore further.

Adishh pov.

Adhya had become my everything; I found myself entirely consumed by her presence. The addiction to her essence was undeniable, craving her every second and needing her constant presence around me. Her smile, laugh, actions, and even her mischievous moments had become my daily dose of joy, and I reveled in the sheer pleasure of experiencing life with her.

I was willing to go to any lengths to ensure she had the time she needed, recognizing the importance of giving her space. This wasn't just about physical proximity; it was an emotional need for her company. I found myself eagerly anticipating every shared moment, cherishing her stories at the end of each day as a personal favorite. In those moments, the tales she spun became a profound connection, deepening my feelings for her. Adhya wasn't just a part of my life; she had become the center of it, and I embraced every bit of the joy she brought into my world.

Today she just came running to my flats with full of excitement.

"Adi....... Adi, guess what? We have a new intern in our department, and he's my age! So, I've got a new friend at work."

"Congratulations," I replied with a pale face.

"Why are you congratulating me?"

"Because you're gaining a new friend, that's why."

"You're being so childish."

"Why?"

"Because you're acting like a little kid afraid of losing a friend to someone new," she teased, bursting into laughter.

"Your jokes need work," I said, walking toward the kitchen to grab a water bottle from the fridge.

She followed me, grabbing my arms. "You're special to me, Adi. No one can replace you," she said, playfully hitting my forehead before darting out of the flat.

As she opened the main door, she added, "If he's cool, I'll introduce him to you. We can have a group of four."

"I don't want anyone new in our zone."

"How boring," she quipped before leaving.

Next day in the hospital Shilpa senior research introduce Gowtham for oncology department has a new intern.

"Hii. Gowtham i'm Adhya. I dont call my has a senior because I have joined 3months."

"That's nice. I will be having good friend here."

"That every sweet for you Gowtham."

Adhya helps Gowtham throught out day because she know how that feel being alone and struggling from day one.

"Adhya have you done culture of new set of cancer cells.?" Dr.Krishnan

"Yes sir."

"Tomorrow, get complete report of gut cancer patient's from gastroenterology department and give it to Gowtham. So maybe all your day will be sent in that department before you leave there shouldn't be any pending work." Dr.krishnan say it confirm note.

"Sure sir by all means."

"Hey sorry, you have to do double work due to my side."

"Not a problem, this what we do there and Im enjoying."Adhya's reason for happiness was Adishh, it was Adishh department.

Okay fine then tomorrow treat on me then.

"Hey. No burden."

"I didnt ask for your opinion it was demand."

Adhya laughed at his words and gave double hand tumb ups.

"Hey, my dear ones!" Adhya entered the room, dancing and hugged Adishh and Trishul.

"What a surprise! I can see some charm in this monkey face," Trishul teased, playfully tapping Adhya's nose.

"That's because I've got good company in my department. This monkey won't disturb or irritate these professional doctors any-more."

"Uff. Finally, I get some peaceful mid-days." Trishul headed to-wards the food counter, suddenly receive a kick on his leg.

"I was an irritation for both, huh?" She questioned, wearing a slightly offended expression.

Both Adishh and Trishul playfully wrapped their arms around Adhya's neck, shaking their heads in a mock disagreement.

"No," both said with a childish smile.

"Hey, Adhya, I thought you had finished your lunch already, but luckily you haven't. Sorry, I was busy with work. From tomorrow, for sure, I'll join you for lunch," Gowtham interjected.

"That's fine, Gowtham. Meet my friends, Dr. Trishul and Dr. Adishh," Adhya introduced them to Gowtham.

"Hey, this is Gowtham," he said, extending a handshake to both of them.

An irritated Adishh whispered in Adhya's ear, "I'm hungry, Adhya. I have outpatient rounds. Please don't waste my time. Let's have your food."

"Okay, Gowtham, join us. Both are getting late."

"I didn't invite your new friend, Adhya," Adishh whispered back.

"Adi, how can we let him sit alone for food?" She pinched his biceps.

"Awwww."

"What happened?" Gowtham questioned Adishh.

"Nothing," Adishh replied.

All of them finished their meal and left.

Adhya's pov

I could sense the tinge of jealousy in Adishh because of Gowtham, but oddly enough, I found it enjoyable, almost as if I could feel an underlying emotion of love. Unsure if I had set my expectations too high for our friendship, the idea of my imagination coming true and becoming more than just friends with Adishh made me the happiest person.

As a friend, he treated me exceptionally well. Now, if I could only imagine being his girlfriend, it seemed like a green flag. All I longed for was his love.

To add a touch of mischief, I casually mentioned Gowtham during our conversations, subtly testing Adishh's reactions. In our chit-chats, I sensed his restlessness, yet he managed to keep himself in control.

Then I said, "You know what?"

"Please don't start chanting Gowtham's name again."

"Not that. I have a full day of work in your department tomorrow."

I noticed a glimmer of hope in Adishh's face.

"Fine, I'm free tomorrow. I'll help you out, and we can go together for dinner."

"Sorry, Gowtham invited me for dinner tomorrow."

The light in his face dimmed once again.

"Promise, I won't stay too late. I'll be back soon, and you'll drop me and pick me up," I assured him, knowing he wouldn't let me have dinner with a stranger or a one-day friend.

"Okay," he replied with a mild smile.

"Hellooooo!" Adhya came running to Adishh's department.

"What are you doing here?" Trishul questioned.

"Today I have work in the gastroenterology department!" Adhya exclaimed with excitement.

"What, the whole day in this department?"

"Yes, yes."

"Sorry, I have an operation tomorrow, so you catch up with Adishh," Trishul suggested.

"Such a busy buffalo you are." Adhya fake-angered towards Trishul.

"How can you say that to me?" Trishul retorted, genuinely annoyed.

"Then what do we call a buffalo? The same name as buffalo." Adhya smiled at Trishul.

"Aadesh, control her, or else she will get a nice beating." Trishul commanded Adishh.

"Ha ha, stop your fighting. I am fed up with your stupid fights." Adishh expressed his frustration.

"Stupid fight," they both said in chorus.

Trishul left, waving towards Adishh and Adhya.

"Come, let me introduce you to my senior doctor, Doctor Rajesh, so you can continue your work with him," Adishh said, holding Adhya's hand.

"Hello, doctor. I am a research associate, Adhya, from the oncology department. I just need some patient history for gut cancer research," Adhya requested Dr. Rajesh.

"Fine, there are some soft copies. Just go through and copy whatever you want, and you can use that chamber as you wish," Dr. Rajesh said with a polite expression.

"Thank you so much for your help. I'll do it ASAP," Adhya greeted.

Adishh joined Adhya to help with her work.

"Don't you have outpatient rounds today?" Adishh questioned.

"No, actually, Dr. Rajesh is looking after today's patients, so I have some spare time for you," he replied with a smile.

"Wow, such a good friend," Adhya said, tapping his shoulder proudly.

"Okay, I'll finish this soon so that I can give this to Gowtham, and we can go for dinner."

"You are so excited about dinner, Adhya," Adishh noted, a hint of jealousy in his tone.

"No, no, I don't have any excitement," Adhya replied, lowering her eyes.

Chapter 8

Adhya pov

As we wrapped up our tasks with Adishh's invaluable assistance, preparing to depart, we unexpectedly encountered Gowtham on our way out.

" I've sent all the files to your email. Just double-check them and inform Dr. Krishnan," Adhya shared with a warm smile.

Gowtham responded appreciatively, saying, "That's so sweet of you, Adhya."

However, Adishh couldn't conceal the intensity in his gaze as he stared at Gowtham, a silent fire burning in his eyes.

"Hey Adishh, we're planning dinner tonight. It would be great if you could join us," Gowtham extended the invitation.

"Sorry, I don't prefer restaurant food. You carry on. Just drop the location, I'll drop both," Adishh replied, his expression unwavering.

Gowtham persisted, "No, no. I own a bike, and I think you're comfortable with bikes, Adhya."

"She's not," Adishh answered with a glare.

"Come on, Adhya, a bike ride will be fun," Gowtham said with a slight pout.

Adhya nodded, displaying a positive sign, and then turned to Adishh with a apologetic look.

As we departed, I couldn't help but notice the flames of jealousy burning in Adishh's eyes.

"It was a delightful dinner, Gowtham. Thank you for that," Adhya expressed while dialing Adishh.

"My pleasure. Whom are you calling?" Gowtham inquired.

"Adishh, to pick me up."

"Why trouble him? I can drop you on my way."

"It's okay; Adishh will be free this time."

By then Adishh already picked Adhya's call "Adhya, I'm picking you up. Just send me the location."

Before Adhya could respond, Gowtham swiftly took the phone. "Doctor sir, why so possessive? I won't kidnap her. I promise to drop her safely," he said and disconnected the call.

Adhya looked at Gowtham with confusion and questioned him, "Why, Gowtham?"

"Chill, Adhya," he replied, pulling her towards the parking lot, holding her hand.

"Is this your apartment? It's nice," Gowtham complimented.

Adishh join us over casually."You both stay in the same apartment?" Gowtham asked.

"Yes, Gowtham," Adishh answered proudly.

"It's getting late; you should leave, I hope," Adishh smirked towards Gowtham. I nudged him with my foot for a subtle signal.

"Come home. I'll make you a cup of coffee," I offered.

However, Gowtham sensed an unusual vibe from Adishh.

"Some other day. Adhya, I'm getting late. Bye," he greeted and left.

In the elevator,

"Don't you think you overreacted today?" Adhya questioned with a hint of anger, but Adishh remained silent.

"Speak up. Don't think you can escape your silence. What might he have thought about?"

"You acted as if I'm an innocent, dumb-headed girl."

"With all that possessiveness."

As we reached the hallway, I seized his wrist and shot him a glare. However, in a sudden, mesmerizing move, he gracefully twisted his hand, enveloped my waist, effortlessly lifted me with one hand, and carried me into his flat. He closed the main door, pinning me against it, with one hand resting gently on my waist and the other finding support from the door, creating an intimate moment that left me breathless.

I lost control over my breath, and the rhythmic thud of my heart echoed in my ears. With a deep inhalation, I finally managed to open my mouth.

"What are you doing, Adishh?"

"I don't like anyone showing interest in what's already mine," he said with a deep, resonant voice.

A shiver ran through my body.

"What does that mean?" Before I could complete my sentence, my body froze, captivated by his unexpected yet enticing gesture.

Returning to my reality, I felt the warmth of his lips gently pressing against mine. In the midst of the tender kiss, my inexperience held me back from fully responding, a regret that lingered. Suddenly, he playfully nibbled my lips. Our passionate embrace led us to the sofa, where he gently guided me to sit on the headrest, momentarily breaking our kiss. As our foreheads met, an intimate connection formed, deepening the romantic atmosphere between us.

He kissed my neck in a matter of seconds, curled his tongue around it, and barely made any deep impressions on my flesh by sucking it. In a husky voice.

"Dont dare to cover your love bite marks tomorrow let all your male friend get a knowledge about relationship status."

I remain silent.

"Speak up, dont escape from your silence." He is repeating what I said earlier.

I nodded at him, my cheeks ablaze with a fervent blush, as if they were painted in the hues of an ardent passion.

After release me from his grip, he hand me water bottle and signed to drink. But my mind was out of control, I just ran from his flat.

Suddenly closing my flat door, I leaned against it, caressing my lips with a nostalgic smile, reliving the enchantment of my first kiss. The warmth of that moment lingered, and my cheeks retained the sweet blush of that cherished memory.

Adishh pov.

Yes, I've kissed her, unspoken confessions hanging in the air. Today, the palpable reciprocity of love from Adhya revealed itself. The kiss, perhaps spurred by my jealousy, held an unspoken urgency – a declaration that losing her from my world was not an option. The days of delaying my love confession stemmed from the fear of losing her, a fear intensified by Gowtham's constant presence. It became clear that the risk of losing her completely outweighed the hesitation that held me back for so long.

In the gentle haven of her response to my kiss, where no barriers or defenses stood, her true emotions shone brightly. The delicate dance of her fingers in my hair painted a vivid picture of passion intertwined with love. A sense of remorse washes over me for delaying the expression of my love, and the subtle blush on her cheeks becomes a poignant reminder. It's as if that blush shattered the last traces of hesitation, compelling me to articulate my feelings. So here it is: she is unequivocally mine—bound by an eternal promise. I cannot fathom letting her step away from my world, as the thought of losing her evokes a fear rooted in a beautiful addiction to her very essence.

Chapter 9

Adhya pov

I received a message from Adishh stating, "You will be taking leave, and it's final." Concerned, I called him immediately.

"Adishh, I can't just take leave like that. You know my commitments to Dr. Krishnan's project."

He replied, his voice tinged with sadness, "You have time to go to dinner with Gowtham but can't spare time for me."

Hearing the disappointment in his voice, I realized the importance of balancing professional and personal life.

"Alright, Baba, I'll manage it," I said, my voice softening. "Whats the plan now."

"Surprise, be ready by 10am tomorrow." He disconnected call.

In the car, Adishh drove towards an undisclosed destination, framing it as a surprise. Tension lingered between us, a delicate shyness stemming from yesterday's intimate encounter.

Obediently, I revealed the love bite he had left, which I had left uncovered at his request.

"See, I haven't hidden your artwork with any makeup," I said with a hint of playfulness.

Suddenly, he applied the brakes, bringing the car to a jarring halt. He turned to me, his eyes wide with astonishment.

"You really took my words to heart," he said, a mix of surprise and admiration in his voice.

I nodded, smiling softly. "Yes, of course." His smile broadened, a silent acknowledgment of our deepening connection.

He led me to the bustling market where we had once roamed with Trishul, our first excursion together etched in memory. Amidst the vibrant stalls, an elderly flower vendor extended a beautiful bouquet towards me. With a twinkle in her eye, she said, "This is from your husband."

"Thank you, aunty," I replied, my smile broadening, touched by the gesture.

Next, we approached the familiar pani puri stall. The vendor, with a knowing grin, handed me a gift box. "This is from your guy," he said, nodding towards him. My smile widened as I took the box, feeling a flutter of excitement.

Lastly, at the cotton candy stand, the vendor handed me a slip of paper with an address written on it.

Holding the piece of paper with the mysterious address, I turned to him with a mix of curiosity and excitement in my eyes.

"Find the location and lead me" he said, handing paper to me.

"Can you find this place and take us there?" My voice was playful yet expectant.

We finally arrived at our destination, a tranquil place situated far from the hustle and bustle of the city, deep within a forest area. The surroundings were dominated by an endless stretch of trees, creating a peaceful, secluded atmosphere. As we walked for a few minutes amidst this natural setting, a charming sight unfolded before us. There stood a solitary house, encircled by a lush, well-maintained garden and open fields. The house itself bore the distinctive characteristics of traditional Indian architecture, making it strikingly beautiful and unique. This picturesque setting was a blend of natural beauty and cultural elegance, truly a sight to behold.

As we entered, the house revealed a stunning transformation. The walls were adorned with numerous photos of us, capturing moments I didn't even realize had been photographed. The rooms were decorated with flowers and an assortment of charming trinkets, creating an ambiance of romance that took me by surprise. I couldn't help but wonder how this introverted soul, Adishh, had managed to create such a heartfelt and romantic setting.

Teasingly, I asked him, "From where did you copy this idea?"

Adishh replied with a playful pout, "Hello madam, for this, I haven't slept all night yesterday."

As we stepped into the living area, I was greeted by a beautifully decorated table, crowned with an elegant cake. Curious, I approached the table, where a collection of pictures caught my eye.

"What are these?" I asked, intrigued.

"Our future," Adishh replied, picking up a picture that depicted a boy proposing to a girl. I turned to him, my eyes wide with surprise. He gently urged me to open the gift box I was holding. Inside, I found a pair of couple rings, a symbol of connection and commitment.

In that moment, Adishh knelt down, and my eyes welled up with tears, a mixture of joy and overwhelming love.

He began, his voice earnest, "I know I'm not the most exciting person, but with you, I feel extraordinary. You've taught me what it means to be possessive, to care deeply. You are my selfish point, the one thing I can't help but put first. I hesitated to confess my love because I feared losing you, but now I'm certain that we are meant to be together, never to part."

As his heartfelt confession filled the room, my tears flowed freely, and I began to cry loudly. Seeing this, Adishh panicked slightly, "I'm not pressuring you. If your answer is no, I'll still be happy just being your friend," he said, holding my hands reassuringly.

Through my tears, I shook my head, signaling that it wasn't a rejection.

"Then what's wrong? Do you have feelings for someone else?" he asked, his voice tinged with sadness. Again, I shook my head.

"Why are you crying, then?" he asked, gently cupping my cheeks.

Between sobs, I managed to express, "I'm just so touched by your words and effort."

The room was charged with emotion, the air thick with a blend of nervous anticipation and heartfelt love. In that moment, the simplicity of our surroundings was transformed into a canvas of deep affection, painting a moment that would forever be etched in our hearts.

In an unexpected, tender gesture, Adishh pulled me into a hug, his lips softly kissing the crown of my head. "Thank you, thank you so much, Adhya. I will cherish your love forever," he whispered, his voice filled with genuine gratitude and love.

As I looked up into his eyes, he gently wiped away my tears, his touch as reassuring as his gaze. "I love you," he confessed, his words simple yet laden with profound emotion.

Blushing, with a smile that reflected my inner joy, I shyly hid my face in his chest. He responded by wrapping his arms even tighter around me, creating a cocoon of warmth and affection.

We immersed ourselves in each picture on the table, each frame telling a story of love's evolution. From the tender acceptance of a proposal to the warmth of shared moments, marriage vows exchanged, the joy of children, and the graceful dance of growing old together, every snapshot painted a vivid prediction of our future.

In that collection of images, we glimpsed the roadmap of a love story yet to unfold-the promise of a shared journey through the ages, culminating in the serene beauty of sitting together, surrounded by the laughter of grandchildren.

It wasn't just pictures; it was a mosaic of dreams, an artful portrayal of a future intertwined with love, creating a narrative that whispered promises of a lifetime together.

"Do you like it?" he asked, his voice tinged with a hopeful vulnerability.

Overwhelmed by the depth of his gesture, I nodded, unable to articulate just how much his efforts meant to me. Our eyes met again, speaking volumes in the silence.

Then, as I glanced around, taking in every detail of the thoughtfully decorated space, I noticed a small tag hidden in a corner: 'Decoration credits go to Trishul and gang.' This discovery added another layer to the moment, highlighting the collective effort of his friends to create this perfect, romantic setting for us.

"Trishul?" I exclaimed, my voice filled with astonishment. It dawned on me that this was more than just a surprise; it was a meticulously planned, romantic proposal orchestrated by Adishh with a little help from his friends. The realization filled the room with an even deeper sense of love and anticipation.

"He helped me execute it, but the entire theme and plan were my creation," Adishh tried to convince me, looking earnestly into my eyes.

In response, I smiled at him, reassured by the sincerity in his words.

"Whose house is this, Adishh?" I questioned.

"It's our own property, though no one currently resides here. But, I envision this as our family vacation spot. It's my favorite retreat, and I've dreamt of spending not just leisurely breaks but even our retired life here. Are you okay with that?" he explained.

A smile played on my lips, "Yes, of course, Adishh. I love this place; it's absolutely beautiful." My response carried not just agreement but the anticipation of creating a lifetime of memories in this enchanting haven he held dear.

Chapter 10

Adishh pov.

It was a day beyond the realms of belief, a moment etched in the stars. Never in my wildest dreams did I imagine orchestrating such a dreamlike proposal for the one who holds my heart, the one for whom my soul harbors an indescribable affection. When she whispered 'yes,' the world around us seemed to pause, and I was enveloped in a euphoria so profound, it felt as if I had conquered the universe itself. In that instance, I realized I had secured a future brighter than any I could have ever imagined. Adhya, the embodiment of my every dream, was now mine for all eternity. With a heart overflowing with blissful memories and a mind swirling with thoughts of our future, I surrendered to the night's embrace, eagerly awaiting the sweet solace of dreams where Adhya and I would wander in endless gardens of love.

The dawn of a new day brought with it a different Adhya, her silence woven with shy blushes, her words hesitant, as if she was navigating the newfound territory of our love. Eager to bridge the gap her reticence had created, I ventured a playful jest to stir the air between us.

"You know, I do have a girlfriend, but to my dismay, she's taken a vow of silence. Perhaps, I should seek a new girlfriend, one who radiates the familiar warmth and spirit of Adhya."

Her response came swift, laced with teasing, "Oh, so you're ready to call it quits just after a day, are you?"

Her playful skepticism was a balm to my worries. "In love, there's no such thing as an end, Adhya. Let there never be a shadow of doubt about that," I replied, my words steeped in conviction.

Her jesting took another turn, feigning concern over the absence of my ring, "I see, so quickly the ring is gone. Have you misplaced it already?"

"I have an operation today, so rather than removing it, I turned it into a pendant," I explained, revealing the ring now suspended gracefully on a gold chain around my neck.

Her reaction was tender, a blend of affection and amusement, as she playfully tugged at my cheek. "So sweet of you, Adi," she said, her voice soft, her touch lighter than air, sparking a warmth that made my cheeks flush with a rosy tint.

Before we could step out, Trishul greeted us with a vibrant bouquet, his presence a testament to the joy our relationship had sparked.

"My girl and boy are finally together," he exclaimed, enveloping both of us in a warm, enthusiastic hug. As we stepped back, his smile was infectious, "So, when's the wedding? I can't wait for it!" His words were sealed with a kiss on my cheek, leaving an echo of familial warmth.

Just then, Gowtham arrived in the parking area, his curiosity piqued by the scene before him. "Is someone celebrating a birthday, or is there another occasion?" he inquired, scanning the area for clues.

"No, bro, we're celebrating love. The hospital has a new couple," Trishul declared, nodding towards Adhya and me with a grin.

"Congratulations, Adhya and Dr. Adishh," Gowtham said, his smile genuine and full of goodwill.

Adhya leaned in, whispering, "See, you were simply jealous of Gowtham, but all he wanted was to foster friendship."

I couldn't help but retort, "Whatever the case, the important thing is I proposed, and I couldn't have waited any longer."

"For what?" she asked, a bit louder this time, feigning innocence.

"Dirty mind, for your love," I teased, tapping her on the head lightly.

"Ouch, Adi, that hurts," she complained, rubbing the spot where my fingers had playfully knocked.

Adhya pov.

In the midst of a group meeting, amidst the usual drone of discussions and the looming presence of Dr. Krishnan's stringent oversight, my phone vibrated discreetly under the table. Seeking a brief respite from the potential drama, I subtly checked the message while taking a sip of water.

The screen lit up with unexpected words from Adishh, "What about tonight? Date, babe." The surprise was such that I choked on the water, coughing violently as the words danced mockingly before my eyes.

Dr. Krishnan's sharp gaze cut through my flustered state, his voice dripping with disapproval. "Can't you even manage to drink water properly?" he chided, giving me a look that could only be described as lethal.

Scrambling to regain some semblance of composure, I straightened up in my chair, managing a weak, "Sorry, sir, sudden cough," hoping the excuse would suffice.

"Fine, but try to concentrate on the meeting, will you?" he retorted, barely concealing his irritation.

As the meeting droned on, another vibration signaled a new message. This time, however, I didn't dare to glance down. The mere thought of stirring Dr. Krishnan's wrath further kept me from even contemplating another peek.

After the meeting finally came to a close, I eagerly retrieved my phone, my thoughts still lingering on Adishh's unexpected message. There it was, another message waiting, teasing in its simplicity: "Seems like my baby is busy."

With a mixture of excitement and a hint of nerves, I dialed Adishh's number, my heart racing with each ring.

"Are you drunk?" was the first thing I asked, half-joking, still baffled by his bold text.

"Nope," came his immediate, amused response.

"Then did Trishul use your phone?" I tried again, fishing for some logical explanation.

"No, he's busy today."

"So, what was that message about?" I pressed, my voice faltering ever so slightly, revealing the blush I could feel spreading across my cheeks.

"I was inviting my girlfriend for a dinner date," he said, his voice warm and filled with an affection that made my heart flutter.

"But those words..." I stammered, unable to hide the blush that his boldness had brought to my face.

"Which words, babe?" he teased, drawing the moment out, basking in the evident effect he had on me.

"Nothing, forget it," I muttered, overwhelmed by the flurry of emotions his teasing elicited.

"So, what's your answer for the date?" His voice was soft, laced with anticipation.

"I will," I managed to say, the words barely a whisper, before hastily hanging up the call, my heart too full, my cheeks too warm, and my mind racing with the promise of the evening ahead. In that moment, despite the distance of the call, I felt closer to Adishh than ever, enveloped in a bubble of excitement and romance, eagerly anticipating the magic that awaited us.

Chapter 11

Around 7 pm, Adishh stood patiently outside the hospital, glancing at his watch as Adhya finally arrived.

"Do we have an extra 30 minutes?" she asked with a hint of urgency.

"Yes, but why?" Adishh questioned, a bemused expression on his face.

"I can't show up for my date looking like this. Just give me 30 minutes to change my outfit," she pleaded, a touch of vulnerability in her eyes.

"No need to be this dramatic," he teased, playfully pinching her cheeks.

Adishh drove towards their apartment, intent on a quick refresh. After precisely 30 minutes, he knocked on Adhya's door.

"Come soon, we're getting late," he called out.

"Coming, coming," she replied, and the door slowly opened.

There she stood, a vision in red – an above-the-knee dress accentuating her figure. The pearl earrings framed her face, complementing her opened hair that cascaded effortlessly. The subtle glow of confidence in her eyes matched the shine of her black heels. Adishh, momentarily forgetting to breathe, couldn't help but be captivated by the allure of his girl.

"Do I look overdressed?" she questioned, her eyes reflecting a blend of confusion and a hint of self-consciousness.

Her presence was magnetic, and Adishh, with a genuine smile, reassured her, Absolutely stunning

"No, not at all, my adorable Boo bear. You're so beautiful; I could just gobble you up," he grinned, playfully bending down to her eye level.

Adhya giggled and gently hit his forehead. "Boo bear? You're turning into quite the flirty boy," she teased, her eyes dancing with affection.

"I'm just admiring my amazing girlfriend, showering her with cute pet names and love. No road romeo here, just a good boy in love with my darling," he chuckled, his gaze filled with admiration.

"Ufffff, Adishh, who knew my silent boy had such a cute side! Now, come on, we're getting late for our adorable night out," she said, pulling him along with a playful twinkle in her eyes.

While driving, Adhya couldn't contain her curiosity, "So, what's the plan for tonight? Just dinner, or are you secretly plotting something more?"

Adishh grinned, playing along, "Well, we officially started dating yesterday; I don't want to speed things up."

"Nonsense! I should maintain some distance from this guy," Adhya chuckled, raising an eyebrow in playful mock. "I was asking about other plans—maybe a movie or some shopping?"

He reached for her hand, "Hey, hey, no distance, nothing. I need you by my side all the time, forever, no compromise."

She couldn't help but smile, "So then be like the good boys okay?"

"Okay, I'll be a good boy and limit my flirting to colleagues and patients" he teased.

A mock gasp escaped her, "I will seriously consider a breakup if you take that step," she said, her eyes twinkling with laughter, creating a cute and affectionate atmosphere as they continued their drive.

"Okay, okay, this Adishh is reserved exclusively for Adhya. Now, let's get down; we've reached the restaurant." He graciously opened the door, extending a helping hand for her to step out.

"My Adi is always the best," she exclaimed, thoroughly impressed by his thoughtful gesture. They entered the restaurant, where a corner table awaited, setting the stage for a complete candlelit dinner experience.

The warm glow of flickering candles cast a gentle ambiance, dancing shadows on the tablecloth. Soft instrumental melodies played in the background, creating a symphony of romance. The air was filled with the fragrance of delicate flowers strategically placed on the table.

Their table boasted fine white linen, gleaming silverware, and crystal-clear glasses. The dim lighting accentuated the sparkle in Adhya's eyes as she took in the enchanting setting. It was more than just dinner; it was a scene straight out of a romantic novel, where every detail spoke the language of love.

Arranged neatly on the table were the offerings of their evening:

Appetizers:1. Caprese Skewers2. Stuffed Mushrooms

Main Course:1. Grilled Salmon2. Chicken Marsala3. Vegetarian Lasagna Rolls

Sides:1. Roasted Vegetables2. Garlic Bread

Desserts:1. Strawberry Shortcake

Beverages:1. Sparkling Cranberry Punch

Adhya couldn't help but admire the display before her. "My boyfriend has impeccable taste; everything looks delicious. It's as if you've been on many dates before," she teased, a playful glint in her eyes.

"Never, this is my first date," Adishh confirmed, his words sincere.

"Ha ha, I believe you, but this looks so romantic," she added, acknowledging the effort he put into creating an enchanting atmosphere for their first date. The scene was set for a night filled with delightful flavors and the warmth of their budding connection.

As Adhya indulged in her meal, Adishh found joy in simply watching her. "Don't look at me like that; I might get a stomach ache," she playfully teased.

"No worries, I'm a doctor," he replied, a twinkle in his eye, savoring the moment.

"You have an amazing taste in food, Adi. These food dates should be a regular thing; I want to explore more," she suggested, her eyes lighting up with excitement.

Adishh, addressing her with affection, responded, "Hello to be Mrs. Adishh, I'm still trying to settle down. Look at my budget."

Amid the playful banter, Adhya whispered to herself, "Oh, stop with the sweet talk. I can't control the butterflies in my stomach."

"Hello to be my future one," he responded, "I know about your situation. I'm not demanding fancy meals all the time. If you're running short on money, we have my salary. I'm not that typical girlfriend; I can even pay the bill." Her words carried a mix of sincerity and warmth, creating an emotional and heartwarming connection between them.

As they concluded their meal, a hint of sweetness lingered in the air, matching the warmth between Adhya and Adishh. With a contented sigh, Adhya looked into Adishh's eyes and suggested, "I think it's time to head back; I've got some pending work."

Adishh, sharing a knowing smile, agreed, "Yes, I have a few things to take care of too."

Amidst the subtle hum of the restaurant, Adhya spoke with a tender optimism, "You know, Adi, moments like these make me excited about our future. Balancing work, sharing meals, and simply being together—it feels like a beautiful glimpse into what lies ahead for us."

Adishh, touched by her words, reached for her hand. "Absolutely, Adhya. Our future is painted with these simple yet precious moments—work, laughter, and unwavering support. I eagerly anticipate every chapter of it with you."

With a shared understanding of the journey ahead, they left the restaurant, the promise of a beautiful future echoing in the air as they stepped into the night, hand in hand.

Chapter 12

In the three months since their paths intertwined, their bond has flourished—a blend of growing love, rare disputes, and endless care. Each day, their connection deepens, rooted in understanding and shared aspirations. Laughter and whispered affections fill their moments, painting their journey with joy and promises of a brighter future. In this shared space, their love doesn't just exist; it thrives, symbolizing a rare, enduring connection that guides them forward, together.

Adishh pov.

In the midst of preparing for a complex pancreatitis case that needed surgery within six months, I was deeply engrossed in a patient's history. The challenge was significant, and my focus was unwavering, each detail a crucial step in the preparation for the upcoming procedure. It was during this intense moment of concentration that Adhya burst into my room, her energy a stark contrast to the serious atmosphere. She wrapped her arms around me in a warm hug from behind, her voice light and playful, "Adi, I'm bored. Let's go out."

Her words were like a reminder of the world outside my medical bubble, yet I was too entangled in the web of my responsibilities to appreciate the gesture. Suddenly, and without thinking, I reacted to her light-heartedness with frustration. My stress and fear about the surgery ahead made me snap, "Is all this fun for you? You may be jobless right now, but I have tons of work to do. Just fuck off now."

The harshness of my words was a direct reflection of the pressure I was under, not of my feelings towards her. The truth was, the impending surgery was a source of immense pressure, and the fear of not succeeding was overwhelming. I knew I needed this operation to go perfectly, not just for my own sake but for my patient's as well.

"I'm not here to irritate you, Adi. I'm sorry. I thought you could spare some time for me and for our love," she expressed, her eyes glistening with tears. We had weathered numerous storms in our relationship, but seeing her cry, something I had never caused before, pierced my heart. She apologized, prepared to retreat, but I halted her departure, gripping her hands.

"Give me just 10 minutes," I implored. Swiftly, I packed up my study table, meticulously organizing everything. In that moment, a realization dawned upon me – I needed to allocate time for us. She wasn't just a companion; she was my stress-buster, a source of solace that I had inadvertently neglected. The balance between my professional dedication and personal well-being became glaringly apparent. While the intricacies of my medical case demanded attention, the stress it wielded shouldn't overshadow the serenity she brought into my life.

Inhaling a deep breath, I made a conscious effort to cast aside the weight of work-related thoughts. Turning towards Adhya, a genuine smile adorned my face, and with a hopeful proposition, I said, "I can't take you out, but how about ordering something?

We can talk and watch a couple of series, sound good?" I added a touch of puppy-eyed charm to sweeten the deal.

"Fine, but I get to order whatever I want, and you foot the bill. Consider it your punishment," she declared, a mischievous smile returning to her face.

"Oh, can I tweak the punishment a bit?" I suggested with a playful grin. "How about some kisses?"

"What?" she responded, clearly caught off guard.

"You know, kisses can work wonders in reducing anxiety and stress," I teased, winking at her.

"Shut up and order; I'm hungry," she retorted, playfully hitting my arm.

We enjoyed a delicious meal together, but when she declined watching a series, she shared, "Adi, I understand your dedication to your profession, but it shouldn't come at the expense of your health and mental peace." I simply hummed, acknowledging the truth in her words.

"Adi, express yourself. Avoid provoking my ire," she warned, her gaze unwavering. Torn between not wanting to burden her and recognizing her greater concern for me than I have for myself, I grappled with a delicate dilemma.

In the depths of my contemplation, I carefully expressed, "I understand, boo bear. This case isn't just about my career; it's a heartfelt endeavor for a 14-year-old boy yearning for a chance at life. My commitment to winning is singularly dedicated to him." Without warning, she enveloped me in her embrace, infusing a comforting warmth that momentarily diminished my sense of self, and the burdens of tension dissipated. "Could you stay with me tonight, please?" Though we've spent nights together before, tonight is different—we're sharing a bed for the first time. I don't mean anything extravagant; I just want her close, to cuddle and feel the comfort of her embrace.

"Alright, Adi," she said, planting a gentle kiss on my forehead. Delving into her chocolate ice cream, she savored each bite. As she polished off the last spoonful, a contented sigh escaped her lips. "Ah, it's Sunday – no work worries. I can sleep in tomorrow without a care."

Resting her head on my shoulder and encircling me with a warm embrace, she shared, "Adi, I don't need your entire day; just gift me 30 minutes. In that short span, it's a universe where it's just us, away from the noise of the world, where only Adishh and Adhya exist." Lifting her head to look into my eyes, a soft blush painted her cheeks. With a gentle curiosity, I stole a peek at her lips, evoking a heartwarming blush and a moment of sweet connection.

Chapter 13

Adishh pov

"Let's go to bed," I suggested softly, taking her hand to lead her into the sanctuary of my bedroom. Once inside, I changed into my comfortable cotton pajamas, watching as she chose one of her shorts and slipped into my favorite t-shirt.

"You have a wonderful collection of t-shirts," she observed, glancing at our reflection in the mirror. The way the fabric embraced her figure seemed to catch her eye. "They all seem to look better on me," she added with a gentle smile, her words weaving a simple yet romantic moment between us but I know it is to fast to move futher.

I watched her reflection, admiring the way the shirt clung to her full breasts. It was true, most things looked better on her. The shirt, me, my love. I could only pray that the reverse was also true. That she found beauty and love and perfection in the way she made me feel and the way I wanted to be.

I climbed into bed, opening my arms, and without hesitation, she rested her head on my arms, which were gently placed on the pillow. I wrapped my other arm around her waist and sealed the moment with a tender kiss on her forehead. She sighed, and I smiled at how much trust she'd put in me. I never imagined it'd be like this. I never imagined I'd ever fall in love.

"You're really something special, you know that?" Adhya said, a smile gracing her face. "Thank you for being here for me. For trusting me. For not treating me differently. It means more to me than I can express."

"Hey, I'll always be here for you, Adi. Sure, we might clash and my anger might flare up more than I'd like, but I trust you. I'm proud to have found someone as pure and selfless as you," she murmured, adjusting herself in the embrace, her head finding a comfortable spot on my chest, where a heartbeat echoed with unpredictable rhythms. Adhya understood the significance of that heartbeat and the depth of affection it held.

"I love you."

"And I love you too, my bo bo bear."

A tighter hug enveloped them.

"And Adi, the 'boo bear' nickname may be a mystery, but it never fails to flutter my stomach," Adhya playfully questioned me with an air of embarrassment.

"Oh... it's because it was my favorite cartoon, and now, you're my favorite too." I winked at her. "Do I resemble a cartoon?"

"No, it used to be my companion in tough times, my stress buster. But now, I have my Adhya as my love."

She chuckled, and the next thing I knew, her lips were pressed against mine. My heart melted, and my hands wandered into her hair. When we pulled apart, I saw the tears still streaming down her face, but this time they weren't tears of sorrow, they were tears of joy.

Good night Adi." She greeted.

"Good night babe" I smiled as we both drifted off into the night, her head rested on my chest, her hand placed over my heart, and me holding her tight, never wanting to let her go.

Adhya pov.

In the morning's gentle embrace, the sun's kiss pulled me from a serene slumber, and as I reluctantly opened my eyes, the clock unveiled an unexpected truth - it was well past 10 a.m., a subtle reminder of time's swift passage. Adishh was nowhere to be found in the room.

"He must be studying," I mused to myself, attempting to rise from the bed. Suddenly, the door swung open, revealing Adi with a tray of breakfast.

"Good morning. Did you sleep well, my sweet?" Her grin and enthusiastic voice filled the room, bringing with it a bright smile.

"Hmm, after a week of exhausting work, only sleep can heal me," I sighed in relief, breathing heavily.

"Oh! That's good to hear." Adi placed the tray on the table and assisted me in getting up, creating a nurturing moment reminiscent of a small girl in her mother's lap.

"I hope you woke up early," I said, sipping my bed coffee.

"Brush your teeth first," Adishh insisted, glaring at me, and I playfully rolled my eyes.

"Yes, sir."

"You look really cute when you sulk," he smiled, and I joined him, sitting beside him.

"Shut up," I teased, savoring the delightful coffee - a perfect beginning to a promising day in the novel of our shared journey.

""Adhya."

"Huh."

"Let's get married," his words had the power to make me faint, yet I managed to respond with a questioning tone, silently praying it wasn't a joke.

"What? Are you proposing to me?"

"No, I just want to tell you that I want to marry you someday," his words carried a promise of truth and trust.

"Oh... yeah, me too," my heart whispered, ready to agree if he proposed right there.

"What are you planning today?" I asked, curiosity tinged with a romantic anticipation.

"I thought you would plan something," he replied, glancing at me.

As I refreshed myself and headed to our flat for a shower, I couldn't help but marvel at the simplicity of this boy's personal care routine. In a world filled with an array of products, he owned only a humble body wash and shampoo.

Chapter 14

A dishh pov.

Today, I have a consultation scheduled with Kiran, a remarkable young patient who has been battling a pancreatitis for 14 years. My connection with him runs deep; I took care of him for two challenging months in the hospitals has primary Doctor. Kiran's resilience and ever-present smile, despite the adversities of surgery and medication, have profoundly impacted me. His dream of becoming a doctor, driven by passion and duty, changed how I see our profession.

Three months post-discharge, Kiran is due for a follow-up and a crucial meeting with the esteemed Dr. Rajesh. The anticipation is palpable, as the outcome could potentially set the stage for his upcoming surgery in three months.

Arriving early at the hospital by 7:30 a.m., I met with Kiran's father, Mr. Srivastava, outside the consultation room. Our conversation, filled with updates on Kiran's progress and Mr. Srivastava.

"Hello sir, good morning." And he hug me, I embrace him with gentle and humbleness.

"How are you doing, Kiran?"

"I'm fine sir, how are you?"

"I'm fine dear."

He was 5ft, slim and cute, and the only thing I noticed in him is he lost his hair due to the medication.

"Good morning Dr. Adishh" Mr. and Mrs. Srivastava says.

"Good morning aunty and uncle, how are you both doing? How's everything at home? And we enter he consulting room.

In the consultation room there are 3 doctor, 1 senior and 2 junior and they were talking something before I entered.

"Dr. Adishh, what's the current status of Kiran? When can we proceed with the surgery?" Dr. Rajesh inquired.

"Although the pre-surgical preparations are complete, we need the patient and their family's moral and mental support. Therefore, I've arranged for a psychiatrist session," I explained.

"Dr. Niana will conduct the session."

"But I think it's necessary that you tell them about the complications that could arise. And the risks and the side effects as well."

"Of course, Sir, but we have to do it gradually."

And session begins.

"Hello Kiran, I'm Dr. Naina, and I will be conducting your therapy. So, shall we start?"

"Yes"

"You can ask any questions about the process and anything related to the proceed."

It lasted for 2 hours continues.

I explained him in detail about the process.

After the session was over, I took permission from my seniors to discuss something with the patient and the family.

After the session concluded, we decided to head to the canteen. It was there I encountered Adhya, who also shared a positive connection with Kiran.

"Hello Kiran," she greeted warmly.

"Hello Didi," Kiran responded, using the affectionate term for 'sister' in Hindi, indicating their close relationship.

They engaged in a brief conversation, exchanging a few words that underscored their bond. However, their interaction was cut short when Adhya received a phone call from Gowtham. It seemed to be regarding some urgent matter, as she excused herself and left shortly after taking the call.

After a long and busy day at the hospital, I returned home. Exhausted, I began reviewing the case report, determined that we must succeed in the operation, whether by hook or by crook. Just then, my phone buzzed with a notification. It was from Dr. Naina she have sent a case file.

Amidst everything, I realized I had forgotten to visit Adhya, who might be upset with me. Lost in these thoughts, I entered her apartment.

I was immediately met with the sound of her voice, loud and frustrated, as she spoke to Gowtham. "What the fuck! You cant just handle that minor issue, report it to Dr. Krishnan, and let me know. I'll redo it, but this is the last time, Gowtham!" she exclaimed, clearly at her wit's end.

she ended the call with a firm, "Sorry, can't fix things, Gowtham" before turning around to face me.

Upon seeing me, her frustration seemed to melt away. She rushed over and embraced me tightly. "Adi, I'm just so fed up with all of this," she confided, seeking comfort after the stressful confrontation.

Pressing a kiss to the crown of her head, I reassured her, "You've got this, my dear Boo Bear. If you need anything, I'm right here."

Concerned about Kiran's case, she responded, "You're already stressed; I don't want you to take on more. I can handle it, and I will." She nestled her face into the crook of my neck, and her hair lightly tickled me.

"I'm hungry, Adi," she said, sporting a puppy face.

"Come on, I'll whip up something. How about egg curry and jeera rice?" I suggested, guiding her to the kitchen with my arm around her shoulder.

"Yum, tempting," she replied, licking her lips and settling herself near the kitchen cabinet.

"Speaking of tempting," I teased with a erotic tone, making her blush.

"Adi, you're acting like a fuck boy," she remarked with a coy smile.

As I chopped onions, I playfully responded, "If you think I'm acting like a fuck boy, then I might as well show you how a fuck boy acts." Slowly, I moved toward her, positioning myself between her thighs and gently holding them. Her breath quickened, and a subtle warmth filled the air.

"Adi, let's not play games," she stammered.

"Oh, no games here. I can't take a label without proving it," I asserted with a mischievous tone, embracing the role.

She pushed away and hurriedly exited the kitchen, declaring, "No need for proof; you're just a flirt with a deceptive innocent look."

"Careful not to provoke me; you might have to deal with the consequences," I warned her, but she responded by teasingly sticking her tongue out.

"Tomorrow night, we're invited to a musical night at Trishul's sister club. Remember?" she reminded, displaying the invitation on her phone.

"Absolutely, I'll pick you up at 8. Be ready," I confirmed.

After some casual conversation, dinner was ready. She chose her outfit for the next day, and we enjoyed our meal. Later, with my laptop in tow, we settled down to work as we had pending tasks to complete.

Chapter 15

Adishh pov.

Today Trishul sister has invited us for her club music night. As usual, we both comes home after the work. We decided to have pre-dinner and get ready together.

Adhya makes pasta for us and we eat and then starts getting ready.

"What are you wearing, Adhya?"

"Surprise, know you go and get ready fast." she urged, gently guiding me out of her apartment and towards my own.

I quickly changed into the clothes she had chosen for me the previous day and then returned to her apartment.

"Tada, surprise." She showed me her outfit and her look.

She looked absolutely stunning, wearing a sleek black bodycon dress that perfectly showcased her curves and highlighted her slender legs. The high heels she chose added an extra touch of elegance to her figure. Her hair cascaded beautifully over her shoulders, and her makeup was impeccably applied, with her lips a striking shade of deep red and her eyes gently enhanced to stand out.

"I think we should just skip the party," I suggested, unable to take my eyes off her.

"Do you not like my dress?" she inquired, her voice tinged with confusion.

"It's not the dress. You're making it impossible for me to think straight, Adhya," I admitted, stepping closer to her.

With a playful yet firm touch, she pressed her index finger against my chest. "Your are spoiled."

"Spoil me" I whispered, drawing her closer.

"Stop playing around, we should go," she insisted gently.

"But I'm serious," I countered, my voice low.

"No, we've made plans, and you're going to escort me. I'm not missing the party for anything," she stated, her determination clear.

"Fine, I'm still taking you, but this conversation is not over."

"Oh yes it is. Now shut up and let's go." She demanded.

"Whatever you say, princess."

Upon our arrival at the club, we were warmly welcomed by Trishul and his sister Tanya, both of whom embraced us in heartfelt hugs.

"Tanya, teasingly remarked, "Adishh, it looks like you've fallen hard." I glanced at Adhya to find her cheeks tinged with a delicate blush.

With a smile, I introduced them, "This is Adhya," gesturing towards her, "and over here is Tanya, the ever-enthusiastic entrepreneur," even though they had previously known of each other by name.

Tanya, with a twinkle in her eye, exclaimed, "What an introduction! I'm thoroughly impressed," her words adding a playful flair to our exchange.

"Adhya, it's great to finally meet you, Trishul has told me a lot about you. Please, come in and make yourself at home," she urged.

Adhya pov.

The interior of the club was a sight to behold. It had a chic and elegant look. A grand stage, surrounded by rows of seats and a dance floor, stood in the center of the large hall.

"Trishul, this is quite the surprise," I remarked, as we settled into a spot at the bar counter. Despite the setting, all three of us opted for fruit punches. Trishul stood close while Adishh sat beside me, casually placing his hand on my thigh.

"The credit all goes to my sister," Trishul explained, leaning in slightly with his elbow on my shoulder. "She's the mastermind behind this, starting from a small café to what it is now."

"Am I just a prop for you two?" I joked, nudging their hands away from me. They only laughed off my protest. Despite their teasing, I truly valued their company. They'd earned a special place in my heart, their friendship a source of comfort and joy.

After a while, Tanya called for everyone's attention, as the musical program was about to begin. The crowd cheered loudly as she welcomed the performers, including a renowned classical vocalist, a young and popular singer, and a talented instrumentalist. The performances were spectacular, and the evening went by in a flash.

After the evening started to wind down, a sharply dressed man came up to me. "Hey hottie, can I get your name?" His approach made me uneasy, but I tried to keep my discomfort from showing on my face. Meanwhile, Adishh and Trishul were off a little distance, occupied in conversation with Tanya.

"Sorry," I replied tersely.

"Just relax, babe. I'm just looking to connect with sexy lady," he said, attempting to reach out towards my face. Before he could touch me, I quickly moved away, choosing to ignore him and head back towards my friends.

As I walked past, the stranger called out, "What a cockblock! You should just tell him you're not interested in him."

My heart thumped wildly, and my stomach dropped. Was he referring to Trishul? Was this why he had been standing so close to me?

"Fuck it," I muttered, and headed to the dance floor, eager to distract myself. The music was loud, and the dance floor was packed, but it did little to ease my anxiety.

In the next few minutes, we danced with joy before planning to leave, with Trishul and Tanya present for our send-off. However, at that moment, someone grabbed my wrist – none other than the stranger.

"My dear, sexy girl, you have forgotten to give me your number," he said, his grip on my wrist painfully tight.

Adishh quickly intervened, firmly stating, "Just let go of her hand." He held the stranger's hand so tightly that I could sense his grip loosening.

Trishul's eyes were ablaze with anger, highlighting the perfect example of 'fire and water' between Trishul and Adishh.

"You have already enjoyed two boyfriends without any conflict. I saw one enjoying your thighs, and another on your upper body. Even I can manage with..." Before he could finish, Trishul landed a tight punch on his face, and Adishh delivered a powerful kick to his stomach. These two friends were clearly adept at handling such situations, showcasing their unexpected prowess in fighting.

Chapter 16

Adhya pov.

I was completely shocked when my friend and boyfriend suddenly got into a fight, but I can't deny that a part of me was secretly thrilled by it. Have you ever been in a situation where your best friend and your partner are fighting over something related to you?for your pride. It's a bizarre mix of emotions, feeling both flattered and anxious as you watch the drama unfold right in front of you.

We now know that five of them joined that stranger's party, and I guess they may be their friends. But still, these two, my friends who are doctors, are very good at fighting. I was mesmerized, yet I was tense because now I can't risk my friends' safety. At that moment, Tanya called her uncle, who is the Assistant Commissioner of Police (ACP) in this area.

One of them struck Trishul hard in the face, and I could tell it hurt him badly. But how could his friend stand by and let someone hurt him? In response, his friend charged at the attacker, and now I'm sure the attacker ended up more hurt than Trishul. I hoped the fight would only last for 15 to 20 minutes, and by then, the police arrived. We explained everything to them. They took those six individuals with them and asked us to come to the station for further details.

I saw Trishul with a bleeding nose, and tears filled my eyes.

"Give me your car key," I said, sobbing, as I asked Adi for the key.

"Okay, but why are you crying?" Adi asked as he handed over the key.

I went and bought a first aid kit, then pulled Trishul to sit on a stranger's bike. Opening the first aid kit, I couldn't stop crying, my nose turning completely red from the tears.

"Why is my monkey crying now?" he asked, touching the blood on his face. I gently wiped the blood from his nose.

"I'm your boyfriend; shouldn't you be more concerned about me?" Adishh teased.

"Friendship is more than love, bro," Trishul replied. Yes when it come to friendship and love, friendship matter first, but another reason for caring more about Trishul is he was hurted more than Adishh and Trishul was bleeding, I care both in same way. By this i can asure that Adishh, Trishul and me share every tight bond.

"Shut up and sit still," I scolded them, and I pulled his face but he hissed by pain.

"Ouch, you're hurting me, monkey" he exclaimed.

"Be a man," adishh said.

"Don't be an asshole, Adi," I warned him. And my tears started falling more now.

"Why are you crying, Adhya? It's just a small wound," Trishul asked.

"I was scared. I don't want anything to happen to you. Please be careful; you and Adi are the best things that happened to me," I replied as Trishul hugged me, gently running his fingers through my hair.

"I can't stand someone hurting my best friend, especially abusing you," he added with a fiery temper evident in his eyes and voice.

"That's enough. Now let's go, we have to register an FIR and give the details."

Trishul insisted us drive. He was always stubborn, and I didn't have the energy to argue with him. Adi drive all 4 us to police station.

Trishul was talking to the ACP while I was waiting for him.

I observed some cuts on Adishh's hand. "Does it hurt?" I asked, and he nodded.

"My boyfriend is quite skilled in fighting," I teased him at the police station.

"I've learned some karate in school. You can take a look," he winked.

"I would love to."

After a lengthy one-hour police inquiry, we all went home.I was really exhausted and was just waiting for my bed. Adishh and Trishul bid goodbye and we were left alone.

I was just about to open the door to my apartment, and Adi asked me, "Can I come in?"

"Umm, yes, of course. It's late. Let's have coffee." I said.

"I'll make the coffee," he said as he entered.

He had made a cup of coffee for me earlier and now I was returning the favour.

"It's so hot," he exclaimed, sipping the coffee.

"Yeah, the coffee is hot," I replied."I meant your body, not the coffee," he corrected, making me blush.

"You should rest, it's very late. Let's meet tomorrow, okay?" He suggested, but I wanted him to stay back.

"Yes, we will, but not tomorrow.

"What are you doing? Come here." I said, grabbing his hand and leading him to the bedroom.

He just smiled and followed me."Adi, can you just stay with me?" I asked.We are set our bed together.

"I am feeling a little cold. Can you please hold me?" I asked him.

"Oh, is my boo bear cold? Come here, let me hug you and warm you." he replied, pulling me towards him.

"How are you feeling, Adi?" I asked him, snuggling closer.

"I'm fine," he said, stroking my hair.I was creasing his wound and he hissed by the pain.

"Ouch," he exclaimed."Are you sure you're okay, Adi?" I asked again.

"Yes, I'm fine. Why are you asking?"

"Because of me, you both have borne all this pain, but I'm so thankful to have such wonderful friends in my life that I will cherish forever." And I kissed his forehead.

"It was just a small thing, nothing to worry about. Goodnight, Boo bear."

"Goodnight, Adi."

And then we drifted off into a peaceful slumber.

Chapter 17

A dhya pov.

After a challenging two weeks dealing with legal issues at the police station, Adishh and I managed to resolve everything without our parents finding out. We were worried they'd never let us go to a party again if they knew. Once everything was settled, we decided to make a fresh start by planning a trip to our hometown together, the first time we'd be doing this. It felt like a great way to move past our recent troubles and enjoy some positive moments together, revisiting the places where our earliest memories were made.

While I was busy preparing some food for us, something comforting like chapati and chicken curry, Adi was immersed in his studies, his laptop open on the other side of the kitchen counter. Knowing his dedication to a healthy diet-a habit I'm less strict about-I handed him a glass of fresh carrot juice. Adi's commitment isn't just to his health but extends deeply into his work, especially evident in his tireless efforts on Kiran's case. He's been fighting relentlessly to save Kiran, enduring countless sleepless nights and navigating through the maze of legal challenges. Watching him, I can't help but admire his determination and strength. Silently, I offer my prayers, hoping that all his efforts lead us down the right path, bringing justice for Kiran.

"Thanks, babe. It's really refreshing," he replied, gulping down the juice.

"Of course, it's my homemade speciality," I boasted.

"I'm not even going to ask what the secret ingredient is," he teased, giving me a mischievous smile.

"I won't tell you anyway," I retorted, sticking my tongue out at him.

"What have you prepared for dinner?"

"Chapati and curry. Do you have anything specific in mind?"

"No, whatever you have prepared is fine."

"Are you sure? You can add some extra spice," I teased.

"Oh no, not this conversation again.

"Yes, you can," I persisted, but he just laughed off my protests.

Suddenly, the calm of our kitchen was interrupted by the ringing of Adish's phone. The screen lit up with the name "Jeevan"-Adishh's childhood friend who now works as a software developer in the USA. Like clockwork, every Friday, Jeevan makes it a point to call Adishh, never missing a single week. This ritual. It has been going on since 2 years he is been to usa. Adishh pick the call and put into a loudspeaker.

Jeevan teased him in a playful, puppy-like voice, "Oh meri pyari sona. Mera babu ne taana thaya."

Adish's gaze was fixed on me as Jeevan continued, "Oh sona, you must be tired, I missed you so much." Despite the situation being somewhat amusing and even boys engaging in such playful banter, I tried hard to control my laughter.

"Fuck, Jeevan," Adish said, his voice laced with embarrassment, likely due to my presence.

"Yes, you can, I'm ready," Jeevan replied, unabashedly continuing the tease.

"Jeevan, stop this; you're on loudspeaker, and Adhya is listening to our conversation," Adish interjected, trying to bring Jeevan's antics to a halt.

"Hi Adhya, how are you, my beautiful sister-in-law?" Jeevan said, his voice adopting a more serious tone now.

"I'm fine, thank you, Jeevan. But I have a serious question," I replied.

"What is it?" they both asked in unison, their curiosity piqued.

"Are you both cheating on me? Like, are you dating each other secretly?" I questioned, laying bare my concern.

"Ishh, he is completely not my type. I don't know how you are dating him," I added, expressing my disapproval.

I could see the fume in Adishh's eyes. "Even you are not a good partner. Such an irritating guy, spending my whole life with you would be trauma for me."

"Fuck you, I'm not that bad," Jeevan retorted, offended by his words.

"Then you said I'm not your type. Remember, I'm the one who kept our friendship on the right path," Adishh replied in the same tone. They seemed to forget my presence, engaging in a heated argument like a couple.

"Shut up, Adishh. I'm the one who makes a call every week," Jeevan defended.

"Bro, we are making calls once a week because of you," Adishh countered. This verbal tug of war continued for the next few minutes, and I was done by then, feeling overwhelmed by their argument.

"Guys, are you serious that you're not in love?" I questioned with a confused voice.

"SIL, it's called bromance," Jeevan justified.

Adishh chimed in, "How's your love life, Jeevan?"

"Asshole, I broke up with her last month. Never dare to remember her," Jeevan replied, his tone reflecting a mix of frustration and detachment.

"Sorry, I'm sorry, Jeevan. What happened? Why did you guys break up?" Adishh asked, now with a serious tone, his voice dripping with genuine concern.

"I found that she's cheating on me. I didn't say anything, but I had a hunch. And it turns out, my hunch was right," Jeevan explained.

"Oh no, I'm so sorry, bro." Has they had causal talk for next ten minutes.

"Ok, guys I have to go, it's time to go. Please take care of yourself. Bye, Adi and Adhya. See you soon, maybe."

"Okay, bye Jeevan," We both said, bidding farewell to our dear friend and cut a call.

"Wow, that was so entertaining," I remarked, letting out a soft giggle.

"That bastard has become so emotional after breaking up with his girlfriend. Even his face is becoming more puffy. And his voice is like a puppy, it's like a small kid," he explained, but I was confused about his sudden shift in emotions.

I move towards kitchen counter and placed his empty glass, "He seems a nice guy."

"Nice guy? He is an asshole."

"What did he do? Is he not a good friend?"

"Adhya, don't judge a book by its cover." By saying he hugs me from back.

"Can I stay here tonight?" He asked and his hands roaming on my waist.

"Sure, you can. Know lets have dinner."

After the dinner was over, we took a quick shower together, and then I put on a T-shirt and shorts.

Chapter 18

Adhya pov.

After the dinner was over, we took a quick shower together, and then I put on a T-shirt and shorts. Adi wore his shorts, and as usual, no T-shirt. His lean, athletic body is enough to drive anyone crazy.I was sitting in the bed and scrolling down on my phone, and Adi came and lay down beside me. He started talk about his day, and his hands slowly moved up, sliding under my T-shirt and making their way to my breasts. For fuck sake im not wearing my bra.

"Hey, what are you doing? You're talking about work," I protested.

"I want to feel your boobs." He replied and his hands were still under my shirt.

"But not today, please," I pleaded, but his touch made me moan.

"Adi your act are crazy today."

"Let me play with your boobs. Just 15 minutes. Please. I will behave."

"Okay, 15 minutes. Don't do anything else." I gave up and surrendered myself to his touch.

Adi lifted my shirt and played with my breasts. His touch felt so good, and his fingers gently circled my nipples.

"Do you like it? You have the best boobs, baby. Let me play with them for a while." He whispered in my ear and I moaned.

His touch sent a rush of heat through my body, and I could feel my nipples hardening under his fingertips.

"Don't do that. Stop teasing me, Adi. It's not funny." I complained.

"You are enjoying this, I can see it," He teased and started playing with my nipples.

"It's tickling," I whined, trying to pull away from him, but his grip was strong."Please, Adi. Your time is over. I will do anything."

"No, 10 minutes more. Just relax and enjoy." I sighed in frustration, knowing there was no point in arguing with him.

After 10 minutes, he finally stopped. "Happy?" He asked, and I nodded, feeling a mix of relief and disappointment.

"I'm tired. Let's sleep, and don't try anything, okay?"

"Don't worry. I'm tired too," he assured, wrapping his arms around me and holding me close.

I tried to fall asleep, but the sensation of his hands on my body lingered, stirring up a longing inside me. Despite the fatigue, my body craved him, and I found myself unable to resist his touch. I leaned in closer, resting my head against his chest and listening to the steady beat of his heart.

"Adi," I whispered, my voice barely audible.

"Yes," he replied, his arms tightening around me.

"Do you want me?" I asked, my heart racing as the words left my mouth.

"I want you, always."His lips found mine, and his kiss was filled with longing and desire. I could feel the warmth of his skin against mine as our bodies pressed together, seeking each other's touch.

"But I promise we have sex after our marriage." He kissed my forehead and pulled me closer.

"We have to wait,okay." He murmured, his hands moving lower and gripping my hips.

"I'll be patient, but please stop teasing me." I protested.

"You're the one who wants this, not me," He said, his fingers trailing along my thigh.

"Adi, please. You are driving me crazy," I begged, the need in my voice unmistakable.

"Alright, let's sleep, Boo Bear."

"Yes, let's," I said, feeling a wave of relief wash over me.

We cuddled together and fell asleep, my body and mind at peace, content to be in his arms.

Adishh pov.

The next morning, I was woken by a kissing on her cheek.

"Morning, princess. It's time to wake up." She was looking very beautiful.

"Good morning. How was your sleep?" She asked him.

"Not that bad," I replied.

"I'm hungry," she told.

"Come, let's have breakfast." I got up and helped her too.

We both washed our face and brushed our teeth and then had breakfast together.

"Let's get ready. I'll pick you up and we will go to our hometown."

She quickly finished dressing and i was waiting to pick her when my phone rang. I picked up the call.

"Hello, is this Dr. Adishh? This is Kiran's mother. Please come to our house immediately. Our son is not responding."

My heart sank, and I could see the colour draining from my face.

"Okay, I'll be there."

I rushed to Kiran's house, where his parents were waiting anxiously.

"Mrs. Shrivastava, please tell me exactly what happened." I requested.

"Dr. Adishh, I don't know what happened. We are having breakfast, and then he said he was not feeling well and then he is not responding."

"Where is he now?" I asked, with tone serious.

"Here, come," Mr. Shrivastava answered.

Kiran's lifeless body was lying on the bed. I checked his vitals, and there was no response. His skin was cold, and his pulse was weak.

"Kiran, can you hear me? Wake up, Kiran." I tried to shake him awake.

"Kiran, wake up," I shouted.

But there was no response. But I tried everything, but he was not responding.

"Call an ambulance, immediately," instructed his parents.

Mr. and Mrs. Shrivastava stood there in shock, tears streaming down their faces.

"Please, call an ambulance. There is still a chance." I urged them, kiran has every fucking right to live.

As they called an ambulance, I started CPR on Kiran and kept pumping his chest, but there was no response.

The ambulance arrived, and the paramedics quickly loaded Kiran onto a stretcher.

"Please, save my son," Mrs. Shrivastava begged.

"I'll do my best," I promised, but even I was hope less know.

As they rushed Kiran to the hospital, I kept a close eye on him, monitoring his vital signs and trying to revive him.

However, when they reached the hospital, we set every thing in ICU for Kiran.

"There is no response, no heartbeat," the doctors said.

"Keep trying," i urged them and Trishul accompany me. Though Dr. Rajesh not yet came to hospital.

The doctors kept trying, but there was response now.

"Finally he gaining consciousness." Trishul said

"Kiran, can you hear me? Kiran," i shouted.

"Please, open your eyes, Kiran."

Slowly, Kiran opened his eyes.

"What happened?" he asked weakly.

"Kiran, what happened? Please, tell me." I pleaded.

"I don't know. I just felt very weak and then everything went blank." Kiran explained.

"What is his condition?" Mr.Shrivastava asked the Dr. Rajesh.

"We have to run some tests, but it seems like we need to do surgery asap" The Dr. Rajesh replied

"Is he going to be okay?" Mrs. Shrivastava asked, her voice shaking.

"We will do everything we can, Mrs. Shrivastava. You need to be strong now. We have to run some tests, and then we will know more."

"Kiran, please be strong. We are all here for you," Mrs. Shrivastava encouraged.

And he was kept for 1 week observation.

Chapter 19

Adishh pov.

I came back to our apartment and picked adhya, we planned to take train towards our hometown. But due to kiran sudden health complications we both miss the train and our last option and only option was bus.

"Is everything okay?" She asked.

"Kiran had a sudden break down. The doctors are running some tests. I need to focus on the case now. It's the only way we can get justice for him."

"I understand, and I'm here for you. We will get through this together." Adhya assured.

I hugged her tightly, grateful to have her by my side.

"Thank you, Boo bear. I'm so lucky to have you."

As we made our way to the bus stop, I couldn't help but feel a sense of dread, unsure of what the future held for us. But with Adhya's support, I knew we could overcome any challenge that came our way.

Adhya and I were crammed into a non-AC bus, which was so crowded that finding a comfortable spot to sit was impossible. We found ourselves standing, squeezed among a sea of passengers.

Suddenly, she winced. "Oh shit, my hand hurts," she murmured under her breath.

"Where, babe? Let me see," I responded, concerned.

"Somebody's pressing on my hand. It's really hurting. Adi, do something," she said, her frustration evident.

"It's not my fault," he replied, a bit defensively, raising his hands in a gesture of surrender.

"It is your fault. You're the one who booked these tickets," she countered.

Trying to diffuse the situation, I suggested, "Hey, let's not argue. Here, hold my hand." I took her hand in mine, hoping to offer some comfort.

"Are you feeling any better now?" I asked.

"Not really," she replied, her cheeks slightly flushed from the discomfort.

"What's wrong this time?" I asked, my patience wearing thin.

"Adi, I'm really thirsty. Could you get me a bottle of water?" she requested.

Sighing, I said, "Alright, give me your wallet then."

"Why do I have to pay? You're the one who booked this bus ride," she protested.

"Because you're the girlfriend. It's your duty to take care of your boyfriend," I replied, half-joking, trying to lighten the mood.

"Fine, take it," she huffed, handing over her wallet with a hint of reluctance.

I navigated through the crowded bus to the shop, only to be greeted by a long line. It took an agonizing while to finally get a bottle of water.

"Here you go," I said, offering the bottle to her.

"It's about time. You took forever," she remarked, clearly frustrated.

"Sorry, the line was incredibly long," I explained.

"I'm so tired," she sighed, resting her head against my shoulder.

"Just a few more hours, and we'll be there," I reassured her, trying to stay optimistic despite the exhausting journey and the relentless crowd that showed no signs of thinning.

"Are you tired, Boo Bear?" I asked her, gently squeezing her hand for comfort.

"I am so tired," she admitted, barely stifling a yawn, signaling the exhaustion from our journey.

"I think I'm going to sleep for a bit. Wake me up when we get there," she murmured, already drifting towards slumber.

"Alright, sleep well," I whispered, offering a smile as she closed her eyes and snuggled closer to me, seeking solace in my presence.

As she fell asleep, I couldn't help but gaze at her. Her face, serene and beautiful in rest, stirred a warmth in my heart. Overwhelmed by affection, I gently kissed her crown. Unexpectedly, she woke up, her eyes wide with a mix of love and surprise.

"How dare you kiss me?" she teased, feigning indignation.

"I just love my girl, and I'm sorry," I smiled sheepishly, caught in the act but not regretting it.

"Fine, but just this time," she relented, a soft smile playing on her lips before she settled back into my shoulder, quickly succumbing to sleep once more.

Eventually, we reached our destination, well past the expected time. It was already 11 pm, and both our fathers were waiting at the bus stop, concern etched on their faces due to the late hour.

"Hello, papa. How are you?" I greeted my father, embracing him in a tight hug, relieved to be safely off the bus.

"I'm fine, but you're late," Shekar uncle, her father, remarked, his tone laced with worry but also relief at seeing us.

Adhya quickly jumped into the conversation to explain our tardiness. "So, we missed our train and had to take the bus instead. That's why we're late," she explained, hoping to alleviate any concerns.

"It's okay. Let's go home. I'm just so happy to see you both safe," Shekar uncle said, his smile warm and welcoming as he looked at us. Despite the ordeal of our journey, the welcoming faces of our fathers made all the discomfort fade away, reminding us of the comfort and love waiting at home.

"It's so good to be back," I sighed with a profound sense of relief as I crossed the threshold into our family home.

"Welcome, my boy," maa greeted me, her arms open wide as she pulled me into a warm embrace.

"Hey, maa. How are you?" I asked, wrapping my arms around her in return, the familiar scent of home filling me with comfort.

"I'm doing good, Adi. It's so nice to have you back," she replied, her voice laced with happiness and relief.

"We've prepared dinner. Let's have a meal together," Maa suggested, leading the way to the dining area.

"Yes, I'm starving. The hotel food was terrible," I admitted, the thought of home-cooked food making my mouth water in anticipation.

After indulging in a delicious dinner that only home cooking can provide, the warmth of the meal and the company rejuvenated us. With content hearts and full stomachs, we all headed to our respective rooms, ready to end the day embraced by the comfort of our own beds, under the roof of a place we could call home.

I heard a knock on my door, and it was none other than Advish. Without a second thought, he blurted out, "Are you dating Adhya?" I choked on his sudden question, caught completely off guard.

"Bro, what are you talking about?" I managed to sputter, trying to feign ignorance.

"You heard me right. Are you dating Adhya or not?" he pressed, his gaze intense and unwavering.

"Go and ask her," I deflected, not wanting to lie but also not ready to confirm his suspicions directly.

"Okay, then. I will ask her tomorrow. And one more thing, we're going to the temple tomorrow, and Adhya's family will be joining us as well," he added, changing the subject abruptly.

"Good night," he said, leaving as suddenly as he had arrived.

I couldn't sleep the whole night, tossing and turning as I thought about what he said. The idea of him finding out about our relationship worried me—not because of the revelation itself, but because of the keep shut, and his silence is very expensive. I texted Adhya a simple "Good night" and finally found some peace, drifting off to sleep after the day's exhausting travels.

The next morning, I woke up to sunlight streaming through the window, a new day promising fresh beginnings and unforeseen challenges.

Chapter 20

Adhya pov

I was meticulously arranging everything needed for the temple visit-flowers, fruits, and various other items-as per my mother's instructions. In our household, we hold a tradition that mandates personal preparation of all offerings before going to the temple. This includes cleaning our home, taking a bath, organizing everything, and dressing up appropriately, all to ensure our minds and spirits are as prepared as our physical offerings.

"Laddu, have you prepared your puja thali?" Amma inquired, her voice echoing from the kitchen. By the way Laddu is my pet name in my home and I hate it, my appa started to call me by this name because I was chubby when I was a baby. Know everyone call me by this name even my school friend, thank god Adishh and advish are not aware about this name

"Yes, amma, everything is ready. Could you please check if it's perfect?" I responded, seeking her approval.

After a brief inspection, Mom gave me a satisfied nod. "Everything is perfect, Adhya," she affirmed, her voice warm with approval.

"Thank you, amma. Could you now help me with draping my saree?" I asked, a bit anxious about getting it right.

"Of course, Laddu. Come, let's get you ready," she said, her tone laced with affection as she led me to my room.

Once adorned in my saree, I assisted Mom with the remaining preparations, crafting some offerings for the gods and lighting a diya in our puja room. The gentle glow of the flame seemed to fill our home with peace and serenity, marking the start of a blessed day.

"Let's go, Laddu," amma called out, her voice filled with the excitement of heading to the temple.

"Just a moment, amma. You go ahead with appa," I replied, my heart fluttering with anticipation. Today was special. Not just any day, but the day Adi would see me in a saree for the first time. My stomach was a bundle of nerves and excitement.

I lingered behind, finding a spot to secretly observe Adishh from the window. He looked striking in his traditional attire, embodying the grace of our culture. Yet, he hadn't noticed me. There I was, hidden away, not ready to reveal myself just yet, my heart skipping beats every time our eyes almost met.

Peeking through the window, I saw Adi engrossed in his phone, seemingly oblivious to the world around him. He leaned against the car, waiting for his parents, lost in whatever was on his screen. I watched him, a smile creeping onto my face, thinking about the surprise awaiting him. The thought of his reaction upon seeing me in a saree for the first time sent waves of excitement through me. I wanted the moment to be perfect, for when his eyes finally met mine, for him to see me not just as the girl he knew, but in a new light, draped in tradition and elegance.

Adishh pov.

Eagerly awaiting Adhya, her presence had become my solace. She was my intoxicant, a constant craving. Her laughter, her smile, every facet of her was an elixir to me. She turned the mundane into magic, captivating me wholly. She was my heart's addiction, a joy that never faded.

In the soft glow of the morning sun, there she was, my heart's delight, draped in a saree that whispered tales of tradition and grace. The red and white fabric clung to her form, a vivid embodiment of love's pure essence, mirroring the hues of a South Indian dawn. Her steps, delicate and measured, seemed to dance to a rhythm only she could hear, each movement a stroke of artistry that captured the essence of her heritage.

As she approached, her bangles chimed like distant temple bells, calling devotees to witness the divine. Her hair, braided with jasmine, trailed behind her, leaving in the air the sweet fragrance of devotion. The gold of her jewelry reflected the early sunlight, crowning her with an ethereal glow, as if she were a deity descended amongst mortals.

Her eyes, bright and lively, held within them the stories of a thousand generations, sparkling with the promise of a shared future. They met mine, and in that gaze, I found my world. The way the saree accentuated her grace, the modest blush of her cheeks, and the shy smile that played on her lips transported me to a realm where time stood still.

"Oh, wow Adhya," I breathed out, my voice barely a whisper, awestruck by the vision before me. She was the quintessory image of a South Indian girl, embodying the rich tapestry of our culture, yet shining brightly with her own unique light.

"Thank you, Adi," she responded, her voice carrying the melody of monsoon rains upon the dry earth, refreshing and vibrant. Her modesty in the face of my open admiration only added to her charm, making her all the more precious.

In her presence, I was a lover boy, hopelessly enamored, witnessing the unfolding of a living poem. Her elegance, her poise, and the cultural tapestry she wore so effortlessly left me in awe. She was not just the girl I loved; she was a celebration of our heritage, a beautiful blend of the past and the present, enchanting, mesmerizing, and utterly irreplaceable.

"You look beautiful," I whispered, my voice barely above a whisper, as if speaking any louder might break the spell she had cast around us.

"Thank you, Adi," she responded, her cheeks tinted with a soft blush, a testament to her modesty in the face of my admiration.

Captivated by her elegance, I felt an overwhelming desire to capture this moment, to freeze this perfect instance of beauty and grace. "May I take a picture?" I asked, hoping to preserve this memory forever.

"Of course, go ahead," she agreed, a playful sparkle lighting up her eyes.

As I raised my phone, aiming to encapsulate her radiance, I quickly realized the futility of my attempt. The camera, with all its technology, failed to grasp the depth of her allure. The image, though beautiful, paled in comparison to her true presence. "You look like an angel," I said, awestruck, my voice laced with a mixture of wonder and frustration at my inability to capture her essence fully.

"Thank you, Adi. But I'm just a normal girl," she humbly replied. Her words, simple yet profound, underscored the duality of her charm. Her extraordinary beauty, paired with her grounding humility, only served to deepen my affection for her.

Just then, my ever-playful brother joined us, adding his own compliments to the mix. Despite his kind words, a twinge of irritation flickered within me, not wanting to share this moment with anyone else. Yet, seeing Adhya's face light up with joy at his acknowledgment, I bit back my annoyance, choosing instead to bask in the glow of her happiness.

Chapter 21

A dhya pov.

"Hey, are you dating my brother?" Advish inquired abruptly.

His question caught me off guard, leaving me momentarily speechless. "No, why?" I managed to reply, a mix of surprise and curiosity lacing my voice.

"Then why are you dressed like that? Is it for my brother?" he prodded, an impish grin spreading across his face.

"It's just an ordinary dress, not meant for anyone. And honestly, he's not my type," I retorted, my words laced with playful defiance, hoping to stir a reaction. I just wanted to tease my Adishh at most amd also we both are not yet ready to tell our parents or family about our relationship.

Advish laughed, his amusement clear. "My last hope for my brother's romantic prospects is now officially dead," he joked, shaking his head in mock despair.

"Do I look like a lab rat, to trail and error method in your brothers love relation." I tied my hand on my chest.

"Please, I'm the perfect catch for any girl. Just look at this," he boasted with a cocky smile, gesturing to himself as if presenting a prize. "I'm the hottest guy on the planet, not to mention the smartest. Girls fall at my feet. And my girlfriend? She's the prettiest girl in the world," he declared, his chest puffing up with pride.

"Wait, you're dating someone? Why haven't you mentioned this? Who is she? Or is it just one of those 'friends' dates?" Advish pressed, his curiosity now piqued.

"It's a secret. You'll have to wait and see," he replied, a smug smirk playing on his lips as he shot a knowing glance in my direction. I was taken aback by his bold facade, silently commending his unexpected acting prowess.

"Laddu, are you driving, or should I?" Appa asked, his voice cutting through the air. The nickname 'Laddu' slipped out, much to my dismay, right within earshot of Adishh.

"I will." Appa was ready to bring car from the car shed.

"You know how to drive?" Adi's surprise was evident, his eyes wide.

"Of course, I'm practically an expert. Just hand over the keys, and I'll show you some real driving," I boasted confidently, snapping my fingers for effect.

"But you never mentioned that," he pointed out, a hint of accu-sation in his tone.

"Because you never asked," I shot back, matching his tone.

"You've been treating me like a personal chauffeur," he retorted, his glare sharp.

"Guys, you both claim you're not dating, yet there's a different vibe between you," Advish chimed in, confusion lacing his words.

"Never mind that, who's 'Laddu'? That's you, isn't it?" Adi teased, diverting the topic just as Reema aunty, his mother, called Advish away.

"My girlfriend would have cute pet names,"Adi leaned in slightly, a playful glint in his eyes.

"You're not even my type, so drop the idea," I fired back, trying to maintain my composure.

"Why do you lie? I'm absolutely fucking your type-the best, the perfect boyfriend for you," Adi countered, his words filled with admiration and a sincerity that made my heart skip a beat.

"Laddu, we are getting late." Amma called me.

"Laddu, we're getting late!" Amma's voice pierced through my concentration.

Firing up the car's engine, I carefully adjusted my saree, preparing for the drive. Beside us, Adi maneuvered another car, his family comfortably seated inside. Our competitive spirits were unwittingly set for a challenge.

"Be careful, Adhya," Amma cautioned, her voice laced with a mix of concern and anticipation.

"Don't worry, amma. I've got this. Let's head out," I responded, a surge of excitement coursing through me. I was eager, not just for the drive, but to impress Adi with my driving skills. However, no sooner had we hit the road than Adi cheekily overtook us.

"What the fuck! why'd he overtake like that?" I muttered under my breath, irritation mingling with determination.

I pushed the accelerator, aiming to reclaim my lead, but Adi was relentless, skillfully blocking every attempt. His playful taunts were almost palpable, igniting a fierce determination within me. With a bit of strategic maneuvering, fueled by a mix of skill and sheer will, I managed to surge ahead, claiming a small victory.

However, the triumph was short-lived. Glancing over, I caught Amma's disapproving look, her eyes practically scolding me for the reckless challenge. The mixture of excitement and admonition filled the car, a silent reminder of the fine line between fun and safety on the road.

We reached temple, we done all pre ritual before entering the temple. I was in my thoughts. Suddenly, I heard the priest's voice. "Narayana swamy, please accept the offering."

I closed my eyes, my heart swelling with gratitude. Temples, for me, are sanctuaries of inner peace, calmness, and mental stability. The act of praying and visiting these sacred places is not just a ritual, but a deeply personal experience-my favorite way to connect with the divine. Here, amidst the serene ambiance and the gentle echo of chants, I find the perfect spot to meditate, to quiet my thoughts, and to seek solace in the divine embrace.

Suddenly, a hand rested gently on my shoulder. Startled, I opened my eyes to find Amma standing beside me. "Amma, what are you doing here? I was in such a peaceful state of meditation," I expressed, a hint of shock lacing my words.

"Don't worry, Laddu. The priest mentioned a ritual involving the preparation of clay diyas, meant to bless you with a good life partner in the future. You'll be participating in it now," she explained with a calm assurance.

"Why, Amma, why?" I protested, my voice laced with a mix of confusion and reluctance.

"It's my duty to ensure you find a good partner," she responded, her tone imbued with a blend of firmness and love, making it clear this was more than just a simple request.

I found myself unexpectedly content at the thought of doing something for my future love life, so I acquiesced to my mother's request. "Okay, Amma," I said, a soft sigh escaping me.

"Please bring a small amount of cow dung," the priest instructed next.

"Why, Amma? Why are we bringing that stinky dung?" I couldn't help but ask, my nose wrinkling in distaste at the thought.

"Because, that's what the ritual requires," Amma replied, her voice carrying a hint of impatience, as if reminding me of the importance of tradition over personal discomfort.

"Fine, Amma," I conceded, recognizing the futility of arguing.

We brought the cow dung as instructed, and the priest guided us to mix the cow dung with mud. Despite my initial reluctance, I found myself intrigued by the ritual, a tangible connection to traditions that have been practiced for generations.

Chapter 22

Adhya pov.

Tucking the hem of my saree into my waist, I began the meticulous process of preparing the mud mixture for the puja. Surrounded by both families, the puja was a vibrant spectacle of tradition and unity. Vermilion was applied, flowers adorned the sacred space, and the air was filled with the harmonious sound of aarti. Amidst this collective devotion, I focused on evenly mixing the mud, each movement deliberate, contributing to the solemnity of the ceremony.

"Laddu, make sure to shape 5 diyas correctly," Amma instructed, gently caressing my hair in a gesture of affection and encouragement.

"Okay, Amma," I responded, my voice laced with determination and reverence for the task at hand. I carefully molded the mud into the form of five diyas, each one symbolizing strength and perfection. The act of shaping these diyas felt like a meditative practice, a harmonious blend of tradition, culture, and love, deeply rooted in the fabric of our family's values.

Adishh pov.

Everyone left after her mother had given instructions to Adhya and dispersed, only Advish and I remained. Watching Adhya work on the diyas, I could see the spark of joy in her eyes, a childlike wonder as she played and shaped the mud. Mud stains adorned her cheeks and arms, marking her engagement in the process with an endearing authenticity.

Advish was busy capturing her moments, taking what appeared to be candid photos, though I knew they were fake candid. A twinge of surprise and jealousy crept into me, seeing how my girl seemed to effortlessly ignore me, perhaps even enjoying Advish's company more than mine. It was a challenging pill to swallow, especially after she declared I wasn't her type, choosing to spend what seemed like quality time with Advish over me.

However, letting this slide wasn't in my plans. I contemplated a perfect revenge, something that would make her realize the error of her ways. She needed to understand the cost of overlooking me and spending her time with Advish instead. It was all in good fun, of course; a playful way to remind her of our connection and perhaps spark a little jealousy in return. After all, in love and war, a little rivalry can sometimes make the heart grow fonder.

With Advish momentarily stepping aside to take a call, and Adhya leaving to fetch some water for the mud mixture, an un-expected twist occurred. The tucked hem of her saree, which had been secured at her waist, came loose, and her neatly arranged pleats started to unravel.

"Ayyo, it got removed. Can you call Amma or Reema Aunty?" she asked in a bit of a fluster, concerned about her attire becoming undone.

"Oh, Laddu, you have your boyfriend here. I can fix it," I offered, stepping into a role I hadn't expected but was eager to fulfill. Kneeling down, I carefully corrected the pleats of her saree, ensuring they aligned perfectly as before. Then, standing straight, I leaned in close, wrapping my arms gently around her waist as I searched for the hem of her saree to secure it back in place. Finding it, I took her pallu, lifted her pleats, and neatly tucked them into her waist, restoring her traditional attire to its intended elegance.

Throughout this process, I couldn't help but notice, with a mix of affection and amusement, how my actions had made her blush a deep shade of red, akin to a ripe tomato. Her gaze held mine, a depth in her eyes that seemed to pull me into a world of unspoken emotions. As I was about to step back, her hands gently covered mine, halting any distance I intended to create. There we stood, enveloped in a proximity that felt both daring and delicate, her breathing audible in the quiet space between us. Words seemed like intruders in this moment of silent communion.

Finally, breaking the silence with a voice that carried a mix of command and vulnerability, she spoke. "Don't call me Laddu," she insisted, a firm resolve underpinning her words.

"Why? You just used that nickname for me," I questioned, puzzled by her sudden decree.

"Because it's irritating when you say it. Refer to me by my name, or perhaps your affectionate 'boo bear,' but not 'Laddu,'" she clarified, her tone brooking no argument, yet a playful challenge lingered in her eyes.

"No chance, Laddu. It's become my favorite way to address you. Plus, you should see yourself—you're adorable when you're blush- ing," I teased, hoping to lighten the mood.

Just then, the sound of approaching footsteps interrupted our intimate bubble. It was Advish making his way back, and sensing the need for discretion, I quickly stepped aside. She resumed her task as if nothing had happened, but the brief connection we shared lingered, a tender memory amidst the day's rituals.

After completing the diyas, Adhya carefully took them to the temple to offer them to the gods and lit them in the sanctum sanctorum, a gesture filled with devotion and respect. Following the temple visit, both families shared a meal prepared within the temple premises, embracing the sanctity and communal spirit of the place.

The day unfolded with a seamless blend of spirituality and leisure as we decided to explore the natural beauty surrounding us. A visit to the nearby waterfalls offered a moment of tranquility and awe, the cascading waters painting a perfect backdrop for our collective memories. We seized the opportunity to capture these moments, clicking pictures that would later serve as cherished reminders of our time together.

Seeking to continue our day of family bonding, we planned a trip to the theater. Watching a movie together not only entertained us but also allowed us to share a common experience, laughing and commenting in hushed tones in the darkened room.

After the movie, we dined at a restaurant, indulging in a variety of dishes that catered to our diverse tastes. This meal, shared amidst lively conversations and laughter, cemented the pleasantness of our outing. It was indeed a day marked by quality time spent together, strengthening the bonds between our families, filled with activities that ranged from the spiritually uplifting to the joyously mundane.

Chapter 23

Adhya pov.

After returning home, I freshened up, trying to unwind from the day's events. Amma brought me a cup of boost milk, despite my protests that I was already full from the food. But as always, 'Amma knows best.' My refusal fell on deaf ears-there was no escaping my daily glass of milk. After the first sip, I stepped out of the kitchen and made my way to my room. No sooner had I settled in than my phone lit up with a notification from Adi.

"What are you up to? Laddu." -Adi

"Don't call me by that name. I'm warning you." - boo bear

"Sorry, Laddu. So, what are you doing now?"-adi

"I'm drinking milk."-boo bear

"And what if I were there next to you?" - adi

"I'd still be drinking milk with Boost." - boo bear

"Dumbo. Good night." - boo bear.

"you will face convenience babe " - adi

This fellow has gone crazy by saying this to myself I was busy scrolling my phone. But sudden there was some sound in my balcony but I ignored.

Adishh pov.

Fueled by the playful banter and Adhya's cheeky use of "dumbo," an idea sparked in my mind. It was bold, perhaps a bit mischievous, but the thrill of it was too enticing to ignore. Our guest room balconies were adjacent, a detail of our homes that I was about to use to my advantage. The clock read 10:45 PM, an hour when the world quiets down, but my plan was just about to come to life.

With a silent prayer that her balcony door would be invitingly open, I approached, my heart racing with anticipation. It seemed luck-and perhaps a touch of divine favor for love's daring ventures-was on my side; her door was opened. Taking baby step with oin drop silence steps, I peered through her curtains to find her, lost in her own world, enjoying her Boost and scrolling through her phone.

Gently, almost like a whisper of the night, I slid the curtain aside. She turned, her eyes meeting mine, a mix of surprise and curiosity flickering in them. Before her mind could unravel the sudden twist in her nighttime routine, I made my move. Closing the distance between us with a step, I captured her lips with mine. The kiss, soft yet bold, was a silent declaration, a mix of all the teasing, the playful arguments, and the underlying affection that danced between us. The lingering taste of chocolate from her lower lip was a sweet reminder of the moment's impromptu sweetness.

When she snapped back to reality, she dropped her glass on the floor, and the sound it made was shockingly loud in the still night. I quickly pulled back from our kiss. Almost immediately, we heard her amma's voice from the other side of the door, fraught with concern, "Laddu, open the door. What was that sound?"

In a panicked reflex, she gave me a swift kick, not enough to cause serious pain, but certainly enough to make a point. Given the urgency, she then pointed to the cupboard, signaling a hasty hiding spot. "Are you out of your mind? I'm 6'2"; how do you expect me to fit in there?" I whispered back, incredulity lacing my hushed voice.

"It was your idea to sneak in here; now you deal with it," she hissed, her whisper sharp as she pushed me toward the cupboard.

I rolled my eyes, but complied, turning toward the wall and sliding myself as far into the narrow space as I could. I didn't have time to ponder her reasoning, my attention focused on the task at hand. From my position, I could hear her calm herself, replying to her amma's inquiries. "I just dropped my glass. I'm so clumsy tonight, Amma."

"Stupid girl, look, the milk has spilled even on your blanket and bedspread. Let me change it." To my dismay, I realized I was hiding in the very cupboard where the blankets were kept. I could sense her footsteps approaching the cupboard.

Adhya pov.

"Amma, it's alright. It's just a blanket. I'll change it tomorrow," I protested, my words coming out as a mumble as I struggled to get out of mouth.

"Okay, but don't forget to put them all into the washing machine tomorrow," she instructed before leaving the room. As she exited, I locked the door and headed towards my cupboard, where my naughty cat was hiding.

"You idiot, how could you put yourself into this mess?" I whispered.

"You avoided me and said that I'm not your type, also you called me dumbo. My sweetheart," he whispered in my ears, his lips brushing against my earlobe.

"Just be quiet."

I quickly turned around and grabbed him by his collar.

"Hey, what's your problem?" Adi questioned.

"Shh, let's be quiet. Amma might hear us."

"Then why did you lock the door?" He whispered.

"Because it's the only way to prevent anyone from entering. So, I suggest you keep your mouth shut or else you will be in more trouble."

"But I doubt." He said in husky voice.

"You are annoying."

"Am I now?" He asked, leaning into me again.

"Yes."

I pushed him out of my way. And sat on my bed, trying to think of something that would help us get out of this situation.

"What if you pretend that I'm not here? And then I'll sneak out of your balcony," he suggested, his voice soft and sweet.

I thought for a while and then I said, "Fine, do that, but remember not a word or you will be dead."

"Sure."

He quickly disappeared into the dark and I heard the sliding glass door opening.

"Close the door, idiot," I hissed, as he slipped back inside.

"Don't worry, I didn't get out, yet," he replied.

"Fine. Go to your room and sleep."

"I'm not tired." He stepped closer to me and placed a hand on my cheek.

"Yes, I am," I mumbled, my mind going hazy at his touch.

"No, you're not. You are just sleepy." He leaned forward, his lips grazing mine.

"Shut up and sleep," I said, my voice soft.He placed his other hand on the other side of my head, caging me between his arms.

"Good night laddu, before you get ready like today think twice." he whispered and left me alone.

I felt my heart beating fast.Why am I feeling this way? I asked myself, as I lay in bed, thoughts and feelings a jumbled mess.

Chapter 24

Adishh pov.

A I jumped off from her balcony and entered our guest room, only to find a figure sitting in the darkness. It was none other than my one and only brother, Mr. Advish Chandrakanth.

"Where were you my dearest brother, or should I ask what was that busy work you had I that neighboring balcony." He questioned.

"Actually came here to get some spare bed spread but I got a call, so I end up in a balcony." My stupid mouth was stammered in between twice, fuck i'm every bad at lying. He glare at me and took his phone in his hand.

"My brother, doesn't even know how to lie properly."

Fuck man, I was caught. What story should I cook up now, or should I even bother? He gestured with his eyes towards my phone; upon checking, I found a WhatsApp message with, actually, a couple of photos.

(Tried all over to find relevant picture but I could find only these. Use your imagination to picturise the sence and photos.)

It was photos of Adhya and me. The clever guy had seen me adjusting and tucking Adhya's saree and had snapped some photos.

"Hey, Bro," I began, trying to sound casual. "What brings you here?"

He flicked on the light, revealing a look of disappointment on his face. Displaying his phone, the photos from today were glaring back at me, including one with Adhya that was clicked in Bangalore.

"I knew you were up to something," he stated, his voice heavy with accusation.

"Like what? We haven't done anything wrong," I replied, trying to feign surprise and innocence.

"I know you're dating her. Why the need to hide it from me?" His voice was now laced with hurt and accusation.

"I'm not hiding. I just wanted to find the right time to tell everyone. It's not just my secret; it's hers too. She should tell you when she's ready," I explained, feeling defensive.

"When are you planning to tell everyone?" he pressed, clearly not satisfied.

"I don't know, not yet. We've only been dating for a few months. It's not something I want to broadcast. She's not ready either, I suppose," I said, trying to reason with him.

After I shared the whole story with him, his mood shifted.

"Have you ever kissed her? Or even touched her?" he asked, a mischievous glint in his eye.

"Listen, you know I'm your elder brother, and I can break you anytime," I threatened, not appreciating the direction his questions were taking.

"I'm your bro, and I deserve to know," he retorted, his tone now teasing.

"Alright, yes, we've kissed. But that's it," I admitted, deciding it was easier to come clean.

"Tell me the whole story. I don't believe you've been dating for months without more happening. Come on, are you a virgin?" he prodded, pushing my buttons.

"Idiot," I snapped, grabbing a slipper to throw at him. He dodged and fled, only to return momentarily, planting a kiss on my cheek. "I'm going to have a cool and beautiful sister-in-law, thanks!"

I launched the slipper in his direction, but it missed. He smirked, about to leave, then paused. "You forgot something," he said, nodding towards my phone. Sensing his intention, I quickly grabbed it back.

"Hey, you forgot to send the photo to your girlfriend," he teased, chuckling.

"Damn it."

I hastily sent the picture to Adhya before handing him the phone. He smiled knowingly and said, "Don't worry, you're the only one in my heart," before leaving the room.

Adhya texted back, puzzled, "Who clicked these pictures? "- boo bear

"Somebody." -Adi

"Who?"-boo bear

"Advish. He caught us red-handed ."-Adi

"Damn." - boo bear

"Relax, he's cool about it. But my pocket's going to suffer."-Adi

"I feel weird. What should we do now?"- boo bear

"Nothing. Just let it be. He's cool, and it's not a big deal."-Adi

"Okay. And tell Advish he's my BFF cum brother-in-law now."- boo bear

"Really?"-Adi

"Yes."- boo bear

"Now I'm getting jealous."-Adi

"Don't be. I love you. Goodnight adi." - boo bear

"Goodnight."-Adi

"Bye ."- boo bear

Relieved yet still processing the day's events, I collapsed onto my bed, wrapping myself in a blanket like a cocoon, and drifted off to sleep.

Adhya pov.

Tomorrow is my birthday, so I've planned a shopping trip with my amma. Being the only child in my home, my birthday always turns into a grand celebration. I might be a troublemaker, but my parents love me dearly-after all, they don't really have another option, do they? Ha ha ha... But I still celebrate my birthday like a little kid: wake up, take a bath, head to the dining table where amma will have prepared some homemade sweets. Both amma and appa will feed me, showering me with wishes. Then, in the evening at 7 pm, we'll have the cake cutting and gift session, surrounded by some neighbors and friends, followed by dinner. And then, off to bed I go, ending the day on a sweet note.

I had no siblings growing up, but my friends who have younger brothers and sisters told me about their birthdays, and they sounded a lot like mine. A big deal was made out of it, with all the family and friends gathered to celebrate the occasion.

Do I sound childish, let it be. I believe in celebrate your inner child concept. Doesn't it sounds good and peace.

So today I going to buy some clothes and other shopping to it our house tradition buy clothes for every special occasion. Today, I'm heading out to buy some clothes and other items, keeping up with our family tradition of purchasing new attire for every special occasion. Amma will pick up the items we've picked from different shops, while appa and I will go to the bank, make an advance payment, and take the required cash from the ATM.

Even as I earn my own keep now, there's something profound about the way our parents continue to support us. A simple call to my walking ATM machine (dad), and I have access to the resources I need. It's not just about the money; it's a reminder of the enduring bond between parent and child. No matter how much we grow, in their eyes, we'll always be that same child with tiny feet and a heart full of dreams. It's a poignant realization that despite life's complexities, some things remain beautifully simple-like the unwavering love of our parents.

Chapter 25

Adhya pov.

After a long day of shopping, I was sleeping peacefully when a knock at my balcony stirred me awake. Through sleepy eyes, I glimpsed a figure outside and cautiously parted the curtains. To my astonishment, it was Adish. My surprise rendered me speechless; all I could do was gaze at him, wide-eyed. He smiled warmly, stepping onto the balcony with a cake and roses in hand.

"Happy birthday to my love. You're 24 now," he announced softly, placing the cake on my bedside table and handing me the flowers.

"Oh my god, thank you so much. You couldn't have timed this better," I exclaimed, overwhelmed by his thoughtful gesture.

"Thank you for these beautiful flowers and for everything," I said, my voice laced with gratitude as I took his hand in mine, feeling a mix of happiness and surprise at his romantic surprise.

"Can you please put these flowers into vase?"

"Sure," he replied.

I took the cake and placed it on the table and went towards him and took the vase and put the flowers and took a deep breath.

We set the table together, placing the cake in the center and carefully arranging the candles around it. Side by side, we watched the seconds tick by, building up to the moment.

"You ready, Laddu?" he asked, his eyes sparkling with excitement.

"Yes, but this name is not my name. Don't call me by that name. You already know it," I replied, playfully scolding him.

"Okay, but are you ready, Boo bear?" he teased, using his affectionate nickname for me.

"Yes," I confirmed with a smile.

As we both began to sing "Happy Birthday," our voices harmonizing in celebration, the anticipation grew. With the final notes of the song, we leaned in to blow out the candles together, marking the beginning of another year.

After cutting the cake and enjoying a slice, I handed him the knife to take his own. With each bite, we savored the sweetness of the moment, lost in each other's company.

Then, in a tender moment, he drew closer, his hand finding its place on my waist, sending shivers down my spine. "Can I?" he whispered, his eyes locking onto mine, seeking permission for a kiss.

I nodded, my heart racing with anticipation, and he leaned in, his lips meeting mine in a soft, lingering kiss. At first gentle, it soon deepened, igniting a fire within me as his embrace pulled me closer.

Suddenly, the tranquility of the moment was shattered by the sound of my room door swinging open. Five figures emerged, wielding torches and lights, their voices erupting in a chorus of "Happy Birthday, Adhya!"

"Surprise!" they exclaimed, their faces illuminated with excitement.

Their surprise quickly turned to shock as they caught sight of Adi and me standing together. I felt a rush of panic as I realized everyone was coming into my room. My mother's eyes flashed with fury, and my father's disappointment was palpable as he regarded us both with a stern gaze.

I was fucked up.

"What is this Adhya?" Amma shouted at me.

"Mom, it's not what you think," I replied, desperately trying to find the right words to defend myself.

"Not what I think?" she shrieked, her voice rising to a high pitch. "What do you mean it's not what I think? We all saw what you were doing," she exclaimed, her face flushed with anger and tears brimming in her eyes.

"Amma, please, let me explain," I pleaded, reaching out to her, hoping to somehow quell her rising anger.

"Explain what? Are you seeing me? Or are you seeing him? Because I don't understand what you are trying to say," she fired back, her frustration evident.

I felt a lump form in my throat, overwhelmed by her questions. I was afraid to answer, knowing that the truth might only escalate the situation further. I wanted to say, 'I'm not dating him,' but the words caught in my throat, unable to find their way out.

The tension in the room was palpable as Adi stood his ground, his tone resolute as he addressed my parents. "Uncle, aunty, I love her," he declared firmly, his gaze unwavering. My parents exchanged a glance, their expressions a mix of surprise and concern.

"Why do you say that?" Appa inquired, directing his question to Adi while stealing a glance at me.

"We've been in a relationship for quite some time now," Adi replied, his voice steady as he met my parents' eyes.

"It's true, Uncle, aunty. We've been together for eight months, and today, on her birthday, I brought a cake to celebrate," Advish interjected, adding his perspective to the conversation.

"But Adi, what were you doing in the room? It didn't seem like just cake cutting," Reema aunty, Adi's mother, interjected, her voice laced with concern and curiosity.

"Maa," Adi began, his voice heavy with emotion as he struggled to find the right words. How could he explain to his parents, in the context of Indian culture, the situation of being caught red-handed while kissing in their own house?

I could sense amma's efforts to hold back her tears, but they soon overcame her, and she began to sob quietly, tears tracing down her cheeks. "This is not right," appa interjected, his voice filled with disappointment. How could he look at Adi now, knowing the mess we had created?

I stood there, feeling utterly lost for words, my gaze fixed on the ground. I was completely flustered and unable to articulate anything coherent.

"We will not discuss this matter further. Are you both serious about your relationship?" Uncle redirected the conversation.

"Yes, paa," Adi and I replied in unison, affirming our commitment.

Upon hearing our response, appa surprised us all by suggesting, "Then we should start planning for the wedding."

The room fell into stunned silence, but appa continued, "If it's the decision of both families and you both want it, we can arrange a wedding."

However, Adi intervened, "I'm thrilled at the prospect of marrying her, but I'm currently dealing with a serious case that requires my attention. I need some time. I promise to stand by my word."

"But you mentioned marriage. It's a significant step, and we need to take responsibility for every aspect of the wedding," Uncle reminded him.

"Yes, I understand. But I can't rush into planning our wedding because of my ongoing commitments, and I don't want our special day to be overshadowed by any complications. I'm sure Adhya understands this too," Adi explained.

I nodded in agreement, adding, "Yes, I understand everything, and I'm willing to wait for our wedding. However, we must consider the importance of time and plan accordingly."

"Alright, then let's continue this discussion tomorrow. It's late now. Everyone can return to their homes or accommodations. We'll discuss everything further tomorrow. Goodnight," Uncle concluded.

As we began to disperse, amma issued a command, "You'll have to quit your job or move out of that apartment."

"I can't just quit my job abruptly," Adi protested.

"But you can vacate the apartment, can't you?" amma pressed, her intentions clear even without words. I remained silent, understanding her underlying message.

"I'll arrange for a good paying guest accommodation, aunty. Don't worry," Adi assured, stepping in to resolve the issue. She nodded.

Despite the tension looming over us, we still managed to celebrate my birthday.

However, a nagging doubt lingered in my mind. In all my 23 years of birthdays, my parents had never wished me at midnight. Why was this year any different? Suddenly, I received a message from Advish.

'Sorry, SIL.' the message read. 'I asked Adi bro about tonight's plans, and he mentioned he had a meeting. I decided to plan a secret birthday surprise with our parents, thinking you might be disappointed about not having a cake cutting ceremony, especially since Adi was busy. I messed everything up.'

All this surprise was from Advish.

Chapter 26

A dhya pov

After the whirlwind of events on my birthday, I finally vacated my apartment with a heavy heart and shifted into a PG close to my old place. Drained from the day's emotional rollercoaster, I looked forward to unwinding and enjoying my day off tomorrow.

Post-shower, feeling slightly refreshed, I checked my phone to find a message from Adi.

"Hi boo bear," it read, instantly bringing a smile to my face despite the fatigue.

"How are you feeling?" he inquired, his concern palpable even through text.

"Tired, and hungry," I replied, my stomach seconding that sentiment with a timely grumble.

"Good, then let's go out for dinner," he suggested, his message lighting up my screen and momentarily my mood.

"No," I typed back, the heaviness of my limbs dictating my response more than my desire to see him.

"Why?" came his immediate question, tinged with disappointment I could almost hear.

"I need to rest today," I explained, hoping he would understand my need for solitude and recovery.

"Ok then, good night ," he sent, his emoji softening the blow of the denied invitation.

"Good night ," I responded, the exchange leaving me with a lingering warmth as I prepared to sleep.

Just as I was about to drift off, a knock at my door jolted me awake.

"Who is it?" I called out, not expecting anyone at this hour.

"I'm your roommate, Ankitha," came the response, a hint of hesitation in her voice.

"Oh, yeah," I muttered, suddenly remembering the presence of another person in my living space. I opened the door to find Ankitha standing in the corridor, her posture suggesting she was equally uncomfortable with this late-night interaction.

"Where were you yesterday?" I asked, curiosity getting the better of my exhaustion as I recalled her absence the day before.

"Sorry, I had some family issues," Ankitha replied, her tone apologetic, suggesting the weight of her personal troubles.

"Okay," I said, my response a mix of understanding and a silent acknowledgment of the shared complexities of our lives.

"Sorry, I've seen you before but I couldn't quite place you," I admitted, my curiosity getting the better of me.

"I'm a new intern in the gastroenterology department, and Dr. Adishh is my senior. Actually, I'm the one who recommended this PG to him. I thought it was for his sister or cousin, but I had no idea it was you," Ankitha explained, her expression a mix of surprise and awkwardness. Despite her words, I couldn't shake the feeling that something was off.

Adishh Pov

After days of non-stop work at the hospital, I was at the peak of exhaustion. Just then, my phone rang with a call from Jeevan, instantly lifting my spirits.

"Hello, buddy!" Jeevan exclaimed, his voice booming with excitement.

"Oh, my dear friend, what's got you so excited all of a sudden?" I inquired, intrigued by his jubilant tone.

"Bro, I got a promotion, and I'm moving to Sweden for the next year. See, I'm earning, and at the same time, my passion for traveling is being fulfilled," he explained, practically buzzing with joy. It seemed like he was flying high with happiness.

"No way, bro! Congratulations!" I exclaimed, matching his excitement. "I'm so happy for you. So, when will you be leaving?"

"It's all set for a month's time, and I'll be flying to Stockholm as soon as I get my visa. I'm looking for a place to stay and have booked a ticket. So, I'll be coming to India tomorrow, starting with Bengaluru," he explained.

"That's fantastic. Need any help settling down and shopping?" I offered, knowing he'd probably refuse but wanting to extend a hand nonetheless.

"Of course, you have to help. As a doctor earning in lakhs, it's your duty to finance your friend, so get ready with your credit card for the next 3 days," he joked, his mischievous nature shining through.

"Hey, you got a promotion, so you're the one who's going to pay, and you're earning in dollars," I retorted, trying to lighten the mood.

"Don't be such a miser, bro. You're the richest person I know, so I'm asking you for money, and you should be happy," he teased back.

"Fine," I sighed, not wanting to prolong the pointless banter.

"Anyway, spill the beans about your personal life. Are you dating anyone?" he asked, eager for some juicy gossip.

"Well, my parents found out about our relationship, so they're planning for marriage. But I have a major case to handle for the next 3 months, so we're taking a small break before wedding bells start ringing," I explained.

"I see. It's probably a good idea to postpone your marriage, especially for such a big case," Jeevan remarked.

"Yeah, I agree," I nodded in affirmation.

"How did you muster up the courage to talk about your love life to your family?" he inquired, genuinely curious.

"Well, we got caught kissing on her birthday, so she couldn't explain everything," I revealed.

"Oh, wow. Now that's interesting. How did that happen?" Jeevan probed further, clearly intrigued by the story. Keeping secrets from friends can sometimes be the toughest job.

I proceeded to recount the entire incident, hoping to satisfy his curiosity.

After chatting with Jeevan, I freshened up and was about to open my laptop when I received a call from my love, Adhya.

"Hey, love. How was your day?" I inquired, eager to hear her voice.

"Long," she sighed, her tone heavy with exhaustion.

"Why's that?" I asked, concerned.

"Because, once again, it's the same old boring PG life. I miss my flat," she confessed, her voice tinged with longing.

"Are you missing your flat or missing me? I'm feeling a bit hurt here," I teased, trying to lighten the mood.

"I miss my flat because I feel lonely in my own home. But I don't want to admit that I'm missing you," she replied, her words laced with a hint of sadness. I could sense the tears welling up in her eyes.

"To lift your spirits, how about we go for a drive right now?" I suggested, eager to bring a smile to her face.

"Okay, I'll be there in a minute. Wait for me," she agreed before ending the call.

I freshened up and changed into more comfortable clothes. Then, I began searching for my hoodie, knowing she wouldn't have dressed warmly for the chilly night ride.

"Hey, Boo bear, are you ready?" I texted her as I stood outside her PG, my faithful bike by my side, my first love.

Before my message could even reach her, she appeared beside me, weared my hoodie and radiating beauty.

"Yes, let's go," she said eagerly, hopping onto the back of my bike.

I handed her a helmet and took mine, ensuring her safety before we embarked on our adventure.

She loved the exhilarating bike ride, and seeing her happy filled me with joy. It was a magical journey for both of us, filled with the thrill of the night and the warmth of our love.

Chapter 27

A dishh pov.

Since Jeevan had come to Bengaluru, I was fully immersed in catching up with him, and Adhya graciously gave me space for my friend. It had been 5 years since we last met, so we had a lot to talk about, places to visit, and shopping to do. In the whirlwind of these past 3 days, filled with hospital work and time spent with Jeevan, I hadn't seen Adhya. However, I made sure to call her, checking if she was upset with me. After all, Trishul had joked, somewhat cynically, that "you can't trust girls; they might get jealous over boys' friendships too." No offense intended, of course—those were Trishul's words.

Once Jeevan left for his hometown, Mysuru, I planned a full day date to make it up to Adhya. Unfortunately, luck wasn't on our side; she was swamped with a new project and under immense pressure. Meanwhile, our team decided to throw a casual party to celebrate a major thesis milestone. Initially, the plan was to have it at Trishul's place, but due to some unforeseen issues, it got relocated to my house.

I contemplated informing Adhya about the party, but Trishul planted some seeds of doubt in my mind, convincing me otherwise.

He argued his point with what seemed like logic, and eventually, I found myself agreeing with him.

Adhya pov.

After a long night at work, I found myself running late back to my PG. Given the early start I needed at the lab tomorrow, compounded by a week teeming with the stresses of a foreign collaboration, I decided to head to Adishh's place for the night. My lab work had consumed me, and as I prepared to reach out to Adi, hoping he could pick me up, I noticed I had already received a message from him.

'I'm tied up tonight, laddu. I'm sure you'll understand.'-Adi

Disappointed but understanding, I booked an auto to my old apartment, arriving within 5 minutes. I could have walked, but it was already 11pm, and the night had grown dark and quiet.

As I exited the lift on my floor, I couldn't help but glance towards where my old flat was, noticing that someone had already moved in. A pang of jealousy hit me, though I couldn't quite place why. At the same moment, music echoed down the hallway from Adishh's flat, unusually loud for his taste. Curiosity piqued and without hesitation, I quickly keyed in the password and pushed open the door, stepping into the unexpected.

Fuck.

Walking into Adishh's apartment, I was met with a scene that took a moment to register. Adishh was dancing with Ankitha, their bodies close, hands intertwined, moving in sync with the rhythm of the music that filled the room. Around them, the living area was alive with about ten others, lost in their own enjoyment of the casual gathering.

As my presence became known, it felt as though the room shifted into a slow-motion tableau. Adishh's eyes found mine immediately, locking on with a look that seemed to try to communicate a thousand words in a single glance. Ankitha, oblivious to my entrance, continued her gaze on Adishh until Trishul, sensing the tension, hurried over to me, his approach also dragging through the slowed time.

Adishh extricated himself from Ankitha and came towards me, just as Trishul reached my side, both of them looking like they were caught in a misdeed.

"We were playing truth or dare," Trishul blurted out, trying to diffuse the palpable tension with an explanation.

My face remained impassive, unreadable, as I absorbed the scene before me and their rushed justifications.

"I texted her that I'm busy today," Adishh reiterated his message to Trishul, his tone laced with frustration and a silent plea for understanding.

"Fuck" Trishul cursed under his breath, directing a glare towards Adishh. "It was my idea, but you went along with it too willingly." Adishh's response was a sheepish nod, akin to a child caught in a mischievous act.

Standing there, I felt more like a teacher overseeing two guilty students rather than part of their group of friends. Their expressions of faux innocence did little to quell the mix of emotions swirling within me.

Deciding to break my silence, I spoke, my voice steady, "Why did you lie?"

The question hung heavy in the air between us, their eyes darting to one another in search of an answer they could both agree on.

"We planned this casual party but you've been so busy lately... We thought you'd feel bad, maybe left out since you couldn't make it. We didn't want to bother you..." Adishh's voice trailed off, the excuse sounding feeble even to his own ears.

The situation, fraught with misunderstanding and the best of intentions gone awry, left us all in an awkward limbo, searching for the right words to bridge the gap that had formed in the span of an evening.

"Dr. Adishh, calm down, she's just your friend. She won't mind about this party," Ankitha interjected, pulling Adishh back towards the party area."Stop glaring at her, or else she'll start a fire with those eyes," Trishul said. I shot him a deadly glare and moved inside.

"Truth or dare is boring now. Let's play Never Have I Ever," one of the girls on the team suggested.

"What's that mean?" another boy asked.

"It's simple. Everyone will have a glass of juice in their hand. Someone asks a question, and if you've done what's mentioned, you take a sip; otherwise, you stay quiet. And those who sip must justify their answer," she explained. I couldn't help but smirk at the childlike enthusiasm in her explanation.

"You might be bored, Adhya, since we're all from the same department. You only know Adishh here. Will you join?"

"Who told you that, Dr. Ankitha? Adhya is my friend too. She's more comfortable here than you, so please continue with your game and wrap it up. Everyone is getting late," Trishul interjected.

My boys never disappoint me. What swagger friends I have – how lucky I am!

"I don't mind joining, but I'm tired. You guys continue. I'll grab something to eat," I said, managing a fake smile. "Adi, where are my cup noodles?"

"Sorry, Ankitha ate them," Adishh replied with that same innocent expression."What?" My voice rose, louder than intended.

"Yes, I ate them. I was hungry. I'm sorry," Ankitha said, her tone carrying a hint of irritation, as she again barged into our conversation.

"I didn't mind, Ankitha, but I was asking Adi, not you. It's better you mind your game," I retorted, my patience wearing thin.

"Come, I'll cook something for you," Adi offered.

"Never mind. Enjoy your game. I'll have some fruit and eggs; that's more than enough," I responded, heading to the kitchen. I arranged some fruits, scrambled some eggs, and toasted brown bread onto a plate before heading back to the party area.

By the time I returned, several questions had already been asked. Now, perhaps in the 4th round of questioning, someone asked, "Does anyone have a crush on someone from our hospital staff?" Trishul, Adi, Ankitha, and two more sipped their drink.

"Has anyone kissed someone?" This time, Adi, Trishul, and one more girl took a sip of their juice.

"Has anyone ever fallen in love with someone in this room?" the question was asked. Adi took another sip, and even Ankitha did. I noticed a subtle glow on her face, but I couldn't help feeling a twinge of discomfort.

Chapter 28

A dishh pov

"I think we should wrap up the party now; it's getting late," Trishul suggested, offering a lifeline I was silently hoping for. The party had its moments, but I was increasingly eager to spend some quiet time with Adhya.

"You're right, bro," I agreed, nodding in approval of his timely intervention.

"It was a great time; we all enjoyed the party. Thank you for everything. We'll split the bill later," Ankitha offered, as she began bidding farewell to everyone. When she reached me, she gave me a quick, unexpected side hug. I could sense Adhya's jealousy spiking—a part of me was amused by it, though I knew I'd be the one to face the music later.

Trishul, ever the peacemaker, hugged Adhya, perhaps in an attempt to diffuse the brewing tension. Then, Ankitha approached Adhya with a probing question, "Are you coming with me?"

"Why would I come with you?" Adhya's response was curt, mirroring the undercurrent of challenge between them.

"Then where will you stay tonight? Here?" Ankitha laughed, her tone laced with sarcasm, believing she'd cornered Adhya into an awkward admission.

"Yes, I will," Adhya retorted with undeniable swagger, dismissing Ankitha's insinuation with ease.

"Are you serious? You stay with your friends," Ankitha pressed, trying to undermine Adhya's standing.

"Sorry, not 'friends.' I'm the one friend here. Adishh is Adhya's boyfriend," Trishul interjected, correcting Ankitha with a clarity that seemed to drain the color from her face. My stance had always been clear, and I had never given Ankitha any hope for more.

With a small nod, Ankitha was about to leave when Adhya stopped her to whisper something in her ear. I couldn't make out the words, but the exchange was brief.

Finally, the apartment was quiet, everyone had left, making it feel more like home again. Adhya went to freshen up, and as usual, she came back wearing one of my T-shirts and her shorts. Just then, the doorbell rang. I opened the door to find Ankitha. In the meantime, Adhya called out from the bedroom, "Adi, why did you change your fabric conditioner? It's not good." She emerged, sniffing the T-shirt she wore, a look of playful accusation on her face.

"I think I left my PG key here, sorry for bothering you," Ankitha said, a bit awkwardly.

Adhya quickly found the key, handed it over to her, and with that, Ankitha left.As soon as she was gone, I closed the door and, without any preamble, grabbed Adhya by the waist, pulling her close for a kiss, my longing overpowering my restraint. But she gently pulled away, a questioning look in her eyes."I saw someone dancing with Ankitha, and those moves were pretty romantic," she pointed out, her eyebrow arching in challenge.

"Seems my boo sees a reason for jealousy in me," I teased, attempting to lighten the mood.

"Well, you could say that, but it's not jealousy. I simply don't like her," she countered, her eyes twinkling with mischief.

"Really?"

"Yes."

"Okay then, what if I have an invitation to dinner with her? Should I accept it?" I asked provocatively.

"Absolutely not. Don't even think about it," she responded firmly, her playful demeanor momentarily slipping away.

"And would you label this reaction? It seems awfully like jealousy. I thought I wasn't someone you needed to worry about," I continued, aiming to draw out her true feelings.

"But you're my man," she declared, her voice softening.

"I am your what?" I feigned surprise.

"You're my boyfriend," she confirmed, a touch of earnestness in her voice.

"Oh, I wasn't aware we were defining things," I teased, enjoying the banter between us.

"I don't care about labels; I just need to know you're mine," she stated firmly.

Drawing her closer, I wrapped my arms around her waist. "I don't want anyone to come between us. You need to trust me. If there's ever a reason to take a chance, I will, because I trust you too. Now, weren't we in the middle of something important?" Her smile was all the answer I needed.

With a look of playful confusion, she gazed into my eyes. Without wasting another second, I kissed her, and the kiss deepened into something far more passionate. Unintentionally, my fingers brushed her bare waist, eliciting a soft moan from her as we got lost in the moment, momentarily forgetting everything else.

"I think we should sleep now," she eventually suggested, her voice soft.

"Hmm," I murmured in agreement, lifting her in my arms and carrying her to my room, gently placing her on the bed. I lay down beside her, our faces inches apart.

Leaning in, I kissed her gently, my hands caressing her cheek. The kiss was tender and filled with love, slowly breaking as we looked into each other's eyes. She smiled and turned slightly away, and I wrapped my arms around her waist, pulling her close. She nestled into me, her hand finding mine and intertwining our fingers.

"I love you," I whispered, unsure if she'd heard.

But she must have, as her hand squeezed mine in response.

Lying there, holding Adhya close, I felt an indescribable peace. The only thing missing was a ring, which I planned to rectify on our next date.

The next morning, as Adhya prepared for the hospital, I offered to drop her, but she mentioned Trishul was already on his way. Reflecting on the previous night's party, I apologized for any m isunderstanding."I'm not mad, Adi. It's just that I didn't expect a lie from you. I'm not trying to judge you or control you. We both value our freedom in this relationship. What's important is that we walk the path of trust, loyalty, and faith together," She emphasized the importance of trust, loyalty, and faith in our relationship, and I vowed never to lie again. "I promise I won't lie to you anymore. I love you so much," With a kiss on her forehead and cheeks, we said our goodbyes, the promise of our future together lingering in the air.

"Bye Adi," she said with a smile.

"Okay. Bye," I replied, already missing her presence.

Chapter 29

A dishh pov

It had been a month since Adhya moved to her PG. Although I saw her daily, I missed having her around me constantly. The idea of marriage started to occupy my thoughts, especially with the Kiran case nearing its resolution. It might sound selfish, but love has a way of turning into an obsession, and I found myself increasingly consumed by the thought of making Adhya mine forever.

Amid these reflections, I was deep into drafting my thesis paper when my phone rang, pulling me from my reverie. It was Trishul, but his words sent a jolt of panic through me.

"Adi, come quickly. Kiran's vitals are dropping fast. We need to operate him, ASAP," he said before hanging up.

Without a second's hesitation, I grabbed my apron from the back of my chair and bolted out of my hospital dormitory, my heart pounding and thoughts racing as I sprinted towards the operation theater.

All I could think about was saving Kiran at any cost. I was determined to fight as hard as he was fighting for his life; I couldn't give up on him at this crucial juncture. Initially, I had viewed this case as a career milestone, an opportunity to prove my skills. But now, it had become something more-emotionally charged and deeply personal.

As I approached the OR, the whirring of machines and the focused hum of doctors working feverishly to keep the patient alive filled the air. Trishul, standing at the end of the operating table, wore a grave expression. I stepped into the room, quickly donning a mask and operating gloves in a practiced, silent ritual.

The next two hours transformed the OR into a battlefield. Despite our efforts, it became painfully clear that Kiran was slipping away. It felt as though he harbored a death wish, stubbornly clinging to life against all odds. For me, the battle seemed increasingly futile, weighed down by a heavy guilt; this case was under my charge, and I felt a profound sense of failure, as if I had let him down in the most tragic manner.

"Dr. Adishh, we can't save him," Trishul's voice cut through the tense silence, heavy with resignation.

"No! We must keep fighting!" I found myself yelling back, my refusal to accept defeat fueling a desperate determination. I was adamant about saving Kiran, desperate to be the one to pull him back from the brink.

"Dr. Adishh, it's time to let him go," Trishul insisted, his voice firmer this time. My knees buckled as he declared the time of death. Kiran was gone, succumbing to his condition. Amidst the sorrow, there was a bitter form of relief; I had endured another encounter with death, though this one had nearly overwhelmed me. It was a confrontation I dreaded, yet knew I would face time and again.

The OR fell into a haunting silence, the bustling activity ceasing as Kiran's fight ended. Overwhelmed, I stumbled out of the OR, dreading the confrontation that awaited me-informing Kiran's parents of his demise.

Removing the blood-stained mask from my face, I faced Mr. and Mrs. Srivastava. "Mr. Srivastava, I'm so sorry," I managed to say, exhaustion evident in my voice.

"Dr. Adishh, please, tell us there's hope for Kiran," Mr. Srivastava pleaded, his voice laced with a fading hope.

The weight of their expectation was crushing. Having already lost a friend, the thought of going through that pain again was unbearable. Drained, I barely kept upright until I caught sight of Adhya in the corner. Seeking a moment of solace, I knelt down, hiding my face in my hands. Then, stripping off my blood-soaked scrubs and discarding them, I made my way to my office, seeking refuge. Barely had I reached it when a knock on the door echoed, pulling me back to reality. And it was Adhya.

I locked the door from the inside and collapsed into my chair, taking deep, steadying breaths to calm the storm within me. I allowed myself a moment to regain my composure before approaching her. Wrapping my arms around her, I felt her head rest on my shoulder, her body trembling. Adhya was tense, both for me and because of the situation at hand.

"Adi, think like a doctor. He was your patient; it's always a battle between life and death. Doctors aren't gods; they can't save everyone beyond their fate," she whispered, trying to offer consolation.

"Lecturing is easy," I retorted, my voice laced with a mix of frustration and sorrow. "Have you ever faced someone's death, seen their struggle for life firsthand? No, right? I have." As I spoke, my grip on her shoulders tightened unconsciously.

"Adi, it's hurting, please," Adhya winced, her words laced with pain.

Realizing my grip had become too firm, I immediately loosened my hold, my action unintentional. "I'm sorry," I murmured, the reality of my physical reaction mingling with the emotional turmoil inside me.

"You don't have to apologize. You have a lot on your plate. I'll be here when you need to talk, I promise," she said, her palm gently resting against the side of my face. In that fleeting moment, her touch offered solace and a fleeting sense of safety amidst the chaos.

However, our moment of respite was short-lived as the doorknob turned, signaling Trishul's arrival. Stepping in front of Adhya, I faced him as he delivered the news about the Srivastavas' presence, his expression marked by concern.

"I'll join them shortly, but could you please assist me first?" I requested, desperation evident in my tone. Trishul nodded in understanding.

As I made my way to Dr. Rajesh office, where I met kiran parents and explained about all other procedure and made my way to my office, Adhya's image lingered in my mind. The emotional whirlwind of the past hour left me ill-prepared to face Kiran's grieving parents. With conflicting emotions and thoughts racing through my mind, I took a moment to collect myself before confronting them.

Leaning against the sink, I found myself staring blankly at the ceiling, attempting to process the tumultuous events of the day. Yet, despite my efforts, an overwhelming sense of foreboding lingered, as if signaling the onset of a dark, stormy season.

We're all born with a spark of creativity within us, capable of creating something beautiful out of nothing. However, many lack this spark, rendering them unable to recognize it in others. Yet, in my work, I found a place where I could truly be myself, where my creativity flourished freely. I was driven by a desire to make a difference, to leave my mark on the world, and to save as many lives as possible. However, Kiran's death had shattered my inner peace more profoundly than I cared to admit.

Engrossed in work late into the night, I was interrupted by Trishul's call, his voice heavy with tension. "Adi, I just spoke to the Srivastavas. It was heartbreaking," he reported solemnly.

"I can only imagine," I responded sympathetically, feeling drained by the day's emotional toll. "I'll reach out if I need assistance."

After hanging up, I retreated to the bathroom to wash my face and take some painkillers, my hands trembling with exhaustion. With no desire to return home, I opted to stay in the hospital dormitory, seeking solace in solitude.

In the aftermath of that day, I distanced myself from Adhya for about two weeks, needing space to process my emotions. Fortunately, she understood and respected my need for solitude during that time.

Chapter 30

Adhya pov.

It has been 15 days since I last had a proper interaction with Adi. While I respect his need for space, I'm also deeply concerned about his mental health. He's been completely shattered since Kiran's death, having invested his heart and soul into the case. Lately, he's been avoiding me, but I prioritize his comfort above all.

During my tea break amidst a grueling three-hour lab meeting, my mind was overwhelmed—I longed for Adi's presence but resisted the urge to pressure him. Suddenly, my phone rang; it was Trishul. Without a second thought, I rushed to the hospital dormitory. There, to my dismay, was Ankitha, not just in the vicinity but hugging my Adi. However, Adi pushed her away promptly.

"I can understand your pain," she murmured, attempting to soothe Adi, but her eyes darted towards me as he looked my way.

I couldn't contain my fiery glare, fixating it intensely on them without a word.

"Look, you really can't grasp any of this," Ankitha said defensively, trying to defuse the tension. "There's nothing going on; we're just colleagues. I'm here solely as his friend."

"Excuse me? Who are you to vouch for my boyfriend?" I snapped, unable to hold back my frustration. "I know who he is and what he means to me. I don't need your pathetic excuses." By taking long breath "just fuck off from my sight."

With that, Ankitha left. Adi's eyes met mine, his gaze laden with deep-seated regret.

"Why are you here?" he asked, his voice barely above a whisper. I glanced towards Trishul, who discreetly left us to have some privacy.

"Trishul called me," I replied gently.

"I failed, Adhya. Another life slipped through my hands," he confessed, his voice flat, his expression unreadable.

"But Trishul mentioned the success rate of that operation was only 5%," I tried to reassure him.

"But still, there was a 5% chance, right?" His voice cracked slightly, revealing his inner turmoil.

"Yes, but we can't blame you. It's always a battle between life and death in these cases," I soothed.

"I'm going home," he said abruptly, turning to leave.

"Adi, wait," I called after him, my voice laced with concern.

"Can you come over today?" His tone was pleading, almost desperate.

"Of course, Adi. I'll join you in the evening," I promised.

"That's okay, I'll take a nap then and prepare some food for us," he said, a faint hint of warmth returning to his voice.

I quickly finished my lab work, and Trishul dropped me off near Adi's apartment. Upset with the situation involving Ankitha, I wasn't ready to face Adi immediately, so I lingered outside his flat for about ten minutes. I'm only human, after all, and jealousy in such situations can be painful.

Then, gathering my resolve, I decided to knock on his door. I heard movement inside as he approached.

I entered to find Adi lying on the bed, looking utterly exhausted. Setting my bag on the table and slipping off my shoes, I approached him. Adi immediately wrapped his arms around me, holding me tightly.

"You came," he murmured, relief evident in his tone.

"Of course, I came," I whispered back, returning his embrace warmly. I wanted to offer him comfort and support, though finding the right words was hard. I hoped he would open up in his own time. For now, holding him felt like enough.

After a while, I sat beside him on the bed and gently took his hand, caressing his knuckles with my thumb. "Adi, it's okay to be sad about this," I said softly, my eyes searching his for any flicker of emotion.

Adi squeezed my hand back, his grip conveying the effort it took to hold himself together. I watched him closely, noting the struggle in his expression. After a moment, he opened his eyes, tears glistening in them, and my heart ached for his pain.

"I think I might never be a good enough doctor, or good enough for you," he confessed in a pained whisper.

"What does that mean, Adi?" I asked, a note of concern in my voice.

He shook his head slightly, as if to dismiss his earlier words. "Forget it. Let's have something to eat; I'm hungry," he said, changed the topic.

"Okay, sit down and I'll serve you," I said, trying to bring a sense of normalcy to the evening.

We sat and discussed his case for a while, but I could see he was struggling with the topic. Deciding to shift gears, I suggested, "Let's plan something for this weekend. Maybe we could go to that picnic spot near the beach? I think it could be fun."

"I don't know," he replied, his expression still grim.

"Okay, how about we just do a Netflix and chill day here at your apartment?"

"What?" He seemed momentarily distracted.

"Or we could just order some pizza and good fried chicken," I offered with a smile, hoping to lighten the mood.

Adi finally laughed and agreed, the idea seeming to lift his spirits a bit. After deciding, I stepped out and texted Trishul to pick me up and drop me back at the PG.

Chapter 31

Adhya's POV:

Today is the perfect Saturday evening for a Netflix and chill session, although Adi and I both know that we'll probably end up talking more than watching. One of the things I love about him is that he's such a good listener. I had some lab work to do today, so after spending about an hour at the lab, I headed to Adi's flat with some snacks and groceries in tow. I watched a tutorial for a delicious Chinese dish on YouTube that I want to try making tonight. It's an experimental recipe, but that doesn't mean Adi should have to risk his life tasting it-luckily, I'm a pretty decent cook.

As I entered the flat, Adi was engrossed in his PlayStation, which was unusual. For the first time since we started dating, he was more involved with his gaming console than his books or YouTube tutorials. I think this PlayStation must have been a gift from Avish. But my man is a true gentleman; the moment he saw me, he dropped his game controller, rushed over, and gave me a tight, warm hug.

"Hey, did you leave your game running?" I asked him as I entered.

He didn't respond verbally, just nodded and took a deep breath. I hugged him again.

After freshening up, I returned with a change of clothes for him. "I've got a new recipe to try tonight. Would you like to taste it?" I asked, holding up his shirt and shorts.

"Yes, for sure," he replied with enthusiasm.

"Ha, very good. Never dare to say no to your wife," I joked as I moved towards the kitchen, not really thinking about my playful words. Suddenly, he followed, pinning me against the kitchen cabinet and kissing my earlobe. I kept my eyes down.

"Why are you shy, my wifey?" he teased, pulling at my shirt sleeves and kissing my collarbone. Before I could react, he bit my neck gently and gave it a long lick.

I turned to face him and gave him a quick peck on the cheek, but he leaned in for a deeper kiss. "Mmm, your tongue tastes so good," he murmured as our kiss deepened, our tongues slowly and sensually exploring each other's mouths. When we finally broke the kiss, we stared into each other's eyes, and I realized just how much I'd missed this beautiful man.

"Hey, I'm here to cook, not for romance. Stay out of the kitchen," I teased.

"My presence is affecting my laddu" he replied, his voice deep and his eyes smoldering with affection. I was about to give him another peck when he took my hand and kissed my knuckle.

"That's for being so perfect. I'm lucky to have you," he said. I blushed, and he chuckled. As I continued cooking, he set the table and prepared the utensils.

"I'm going to the bathroom," he announced, "Be right back."

As soon as he left the kitchen, I took a deep breath, trying to calm the excitement he'd stirred up. After a couple of minutes, Adi returned smelling of soap, which made me smile.

"You look good," I complimented.

"I just came from the bathroom," he giggled, "but thank you."

"Yes, you do," I affirmed.

"Okay, can we eat now?" he asked, eyeing the food eagerly.

"Of course," I agreed.

"Can we pray first?" he suggested, placing his hand over mine. I nodded, and we clasped hands, bowing our heads together.

"Thank you for bringing us together," he said softly, looking up at me with tender eyes, "And for the food."

"Of course, Adi, it's my pleasure," I said, feeling my cheeks warm with a blush.

"May the Lord bless us with many more blessings," he continued, his eyes crinkling slightly with affection. "I love you so much."

"And I love you too," I smiled as he reached over to cut my food for me.

When we were done, we cleaned the dish together and settled on the couch. Snuggling close to Adi, I ventured cautiously, "How's everything going? I know it's not the best time to ask, but..."

"It's okay. I'm learning, Adhya. I never thought my whole life would someone will die in my hands. I opted for medicine to save lives, but look at it now," he shared, his tone tinged with the weight of his responsibilities.

"Hey, it's not your fault what happened, Adi. And I'm sure you're a great doctor. You still have a lot to learn, and you'll do just fine. Death are pre written." I comforted him, my words meant to soothe. I wrapped my arms around him, pulling him close to ease his burden.

After alive talking about any other things we finally trun on the tv "Let's leave all this for now. Let's watch a movie, okay?"

"Hmm… okay," he murmured in agreement. We chose a romantic film, and as the two lead actors began their on-screen romance, Adi drew me closer. His lips gently brushed the nape of my neck, sending a shiver down my spine. I turned in my seat to face him, our eyes locking and my breath catching. He leaned in for another kiss, this time on the lips, his hands weaving through my hair. After a few moments, I pulled away slightly, smiling shyly at him.

"I'm sorry," he apologized, though his tone suggested a playful insincerity. He pulled me closer again, kissing me more intensely.

After a moment, I gently pulled away. "No, don't apologize. I… I…" I stuttered, overwhelmed by emotions.

He leaned in, kissed me on the cheek, and then turned back towards the TV. I lay beside him, my mind racing. After a few minutes, I realized it was late and perhaps time to retreat. "Hey, I think it's late. I'll go to sleep," I suggested.

"Yeah, I'm sleepy too," he replied. We headed to the bedroom, where I completed my skincare routine and brushed my teeth. Adi joined me after a quick shower and turned off the lights before sliding into bed beside me.

We lay there in silence, my heart pounding as I pondered the night's events. Exhausted yet restless, I needed to talk, to reconnect. "Hey, Adi, can we talk?" I whispered, my voice shaky, hoping for a response.

But the steady rhythm of his breathing told me he was already asleep. I sighed, turning over onto my side, feeling the gap widen even as he slept just inches away.

Chapter 32

Adhya POV:

I woke up around 8 but couldn't find Adi in bed. After completing my morning routine, I walked toward the hall where I found Adi holding some papers in his hand. My body froze for a second, but he didn't utter a word and moved towards the kitchen. He poured some coffee into a cup and handed it to me. "Adi, that..." My words stopped short under his intense, heated glare. Within seconds, my eyes filled with tears.

Gathering my courage, I pleaded, "Just give me five minutes, I will explain everything. Please, Adi." All I received in return was his stony silence.

"Speak up, Adi!" My voice cracked with frustration.

"What do you expect me to say? That I'm okay with this? That it's fine to just drop a bomb like this and act as if nothing's changed?" he replied coldly, his voice a mixture of hurt and disbelief.

"Adi, I...it's not like that. I wasn't going to just leave!" I exclaimed, trying to hold back more tears.

Adishh POV:

How could she not tell me about Sweden? About moving so far away? I felt a mix of betrayal and panic. "And when were you going to tell me? On your way to the airport?" I accused, the hurt evident in my voice.

"Adi, please understand. I was going to tell you…I was just trying to figure out how to do it right," she replied, her voice trembling.

"Figuring it out? By leaving me in the dark? Is that how we work now? Keeping secrets?" I shot back, unable to hide the frustration and anger building inside me.

Adhya's face crumbled, and she reached out, her hand trembling. "No, Adi. I… I thought about it, and I decided I'm not going. I can't go. Not without you, leaving you that this situation, I cant go when your suffering" she confessed, her voice barely above a whisper.

I looked at her, confused and taken aback by her sudden decision. "You can't make decisions based on me, Adhya! Your career, your dreams—they can't just be tossed aside!"

"It's not just about my career, Adi! This is about us, about what I want—and I want to be here, with you," she insisted, her determination clear despite the tears in her eyes.

"And what about what I want? Do you think it's fair to make me the anchor that holds you back from such an opportunity?" I argued, feeling torn between my love for her and wanting the best for her.

"Adi, you're not holding me back! You are my home, and I'd rather lose a job than lose you," she said passionately.

I paced back and forth, raking my fingers through my hair, my emotions in turmoil. "I don't want your sacrifices, Adhya! I can't have you resent me one day for choosing me over your dreams."

"It's not a sacrifice if it's a choice I want to make, Adi! Why can't you see that? Why can't you trust my love for you as much as I trust in us?" She was pleading now, her eyes earnest and full of pain.

"Because it's not just about love! It's about life, about surviving, thriving! Don't ask me to be okay with you giving up parts of yourself for me. I can't do that. I love you too much. But i'm not that selfish dont play stupid game just like immatured one. I dont want your sacrifice in name of love." After taking long breath "if I was in my place I would closed career over you."

"Don't you fucking dare, Adi." She hissed, unable to control her emotions. "You are not going to insult me like this and my feels are not for granted moreover I level my fucking relationship and my loved one's feelings with my fucking life, you think i'm that stupid, yes, I will leave." She was beyond angry, her words filled with a cold fury as she fought to contain her emotions. After a minutes "don't you think that we gonna work on long distance relationship, i'm give a last chance to you if you stop me I am gonna stay forever with you or else your Adhya is gone." After take time she break her silence "Then let me make your choice, Adi." she implored, stepping closer, her eyes searching mine for understanding.

We stood there, a mere breath apart, the weight of her words hanging between us. In that moment, I realized that her staying wasn't just about sacrifice—it was about choosing where her heart belonged. And as much as it terrified me to accept such a weighty gift, I knew I had to step back and let her choose her own path—even if it was one that led her right back to me.As I paced around the apartment, my thoughts churned in turmoil, each step echoing the heaviness in my heart. The weight of sadness settled over me like a suffocating blanket, drowning me in its darkness. It felt like a storm had brewed inside me, raging with remorse and regret.

"Adi, Adi, Adi..." Her name echoed in my mind, a haunting reminder of her absence. She had always been there, a constant presence in my life, a pillar of support. How could I have been so blind, so oblivious to her pain? Guilt gnawed at me, clawing at my conscience.

I collapsed onto my bed, the weight of my emotions crushing me. Each breath felt like a struggle, the ache in my chest unbearable. I had pushed her away, hurt her with my words, and now she was gone. The realization hit me like a tidal wave, overwhelming me with grief.

Tears streamed down my face, unchecked and unrestrained. I curled up into a ball, clutching at the empty space where she used to be. The silence of the room was deafening, echoing with the echoes of my sobs. How could I have let her slip away, let my fears and insecurities drive her away?

Exhaustion washed over me like a tidal wave, pulling me into a fitful sleep haunted by dreams of her. I tossed and turned, tormented by memories of our time together, haunted by the words left unspoken. I wished with every fiber of my being that I could turn back time, undo the damage I had caused. But in the darkness of the night, all I could do was mourn the loss of what could have been.

Chapter 33

F lashback:

They had planned the quintessential romantic escape—a serene lakeside picnic followed by dinner under the stars at a quaint nearby restaurant. The day had been woven with laughter and soft exchanges, the sort that drew hearts closer in silent acknowledgment of deepening affection.

As they drove back, the comforting hum of the car mingled with their contented sighs. The evening air was crisp, wrapping around them like a delicate, cool shawl as they entered their cozy home.

"We're both heading to the same place, how about we get married?" Adhya asked, her eyes twinkling with a blend of mischief and hope. Adi, caught in the warmth of their shared dreams on their plush sofa, couldn't find it in himself to deny her anything. He pulled her close, her laughter mingling with the rustle of her snack bag as she settled more comfortably against him.

"So, what do we do next?" he murmured, her voice a soft caress against her ear.

"Do you want to dance?" she suggested, a playful lilt in her voice.

"No, not really; it's very cold. I'd rather just cuddle here with you," he replied, his voice low and husky, resonating with a warmth that made her heart flutter. She giggled, loving how his voice dipped with each word, her laughter echoing lightly in the quiet room.

"What's so funny?" he asked

Her lips curving into a teasing smile. "Nothing," she replied, a mischievous sparkle in her eyes.

"Adhya," he prodded gently, drawing her closer until their foreheads touched.

"Hmm…" she hummed, her eyes closing as she savored the warmth of his body against hers.

"What made you fall in love with me?" he whispered, his breath tickling her ear. "I know I'm not always the most exciting person. I get so wrapped up in my work, and I worry I don't give you enough time," he confessed, vulnerability threading his voice.

Adhya lifted her head, her gaze locking with his, intense and full of sincerity. "Adi, you may think you're quiet and reserved, but your love speaks volumes. It chases after me, even in your silence. You're dedicated to your career, yes, but you never fail to stand by me when it matters most. To me, that's perfection—a perfection you don't see in yourself," she said, her words painting the depth of her feelings for him.

Overwhelmed by her declaration, Adi captured her lips with his in a kiss that started tender and exploratory but soon deepened with passion. His hands roamed over her back, drawing her closer as she threaded her fingers through his hair, each movement stoking the growing fire between them.

Their breaths became ragged as the kiss intensified. Adi's hands moved to unbutton his shirt, his eyes never leaving hers, asking for permission without words. She nodded slightly, her breath catching in her throat as his lips traced a path down her neck.

"I think we should stop, Laddu," he gasped suddenly, pulling back slightly, his eyes clouded with a mix of desire and restraint. She didn't reply, again he "I promise that we going have all this after our marriage, but right know I regret for my promise."

She touched his cheek, her voice barely above a whisper. "You can break your promise, if you want."

He looked at her, torn. "You're playing a dangerous game," he growled softly, desire lacing his voice.

"Do you not like it?" she teased, a coy smile playing on her lips.

"Adhya, don't tempt me. You might just regret it," he warned, his voice husky with unspoken promises.

She giggled, the sound light and carefree. "But I don't."

"It is," he conceded, a chuckle escaping him. "You're my greatest temptation."

"Let's go to my bedroom," he suggested, his voice now a sultry whisper that sent shivers down her spine.

Her expression sobered. "What if we never get married?"

"Then lets try live in" he replied instantly, his voice tinged with humor yet earnest in his intent.

"And your promise?" she teased back, her eyes gleaming with affection.

"I want all of you, Adhya—not just physically but every facet of you. Your presence, your laughter, your thoughts, and your dreams," he murmured, leaning in to kiss her deeply once more. Their kiss was fervent, their mutual desire palpable as they lost themselves in each other, exploring and reaffirming their love in the quiet solitude of their shared space.

These memories haunted their sleep, disturbing them profound-ly. In desperation, both reached for their phones and dialed at the same time, causing their calls to collide and fail to connect. Frustrated, they tried again, but with the same result.

Overwhelmed by emotion, Adhya began to sob uncontrollably. The pain was piercing, echoing deeply within her. Yes, they had weathered many arguments before, but none had ever cut this deep. All she longed for now was a call from Adishh, a simple gesture that might start to mend the fractures in their relationship.

As she sat curled up, her phone gripped tightly in her hand, Adhya felt the weight of their unresolved conflict. Each moment that passed without hearing from Adishh only intensified her distress. The silence between them, once a peaceful quietude, now seemed an insurmountable void, filled with the echoes of words unsaid and apologies unspoken.

On the other side, Adishh was overwhelmed with confusion and uncertainty about how to mend things. He paced back and forth, phone in hand, wrestling with his thoughts. He wanted desperately to reach out to Adhya, to bridge the growing silence between them, but fear of making things worse held him back. Each attempt to dial her number was interrupted by his anxiety—what if his call only deepened the rift? Torn between action and inaction, Adishh felt paralyzed, unsure of how to heal the wounds that were threatening to pull them apart.

Chapter 34

The above aesthetic just a try, author is very dumb in phone and editing , so just to explore wattpad I tried thats it...... Dont think 'isss this writer is very cringe.' No offense ryt friends.

Okay I know I never interacted with any of the reader, because I very bad at start conversation.

So lets play a game..

I will come up with different games in different Chapter so no boring games. (if this doesn't work, sure I gonna delete this entire conversation don't mind me wrong).

This Chapter game is guess the truth.(hint: there are multiple truth too)

1. Writer is aged under 18.2. Writer is doesn't know how to drive any of the vehicles.3. Writer is state level basketball player.4. I was caught with parents while discussing about LGBTQ+ topic with my friends.5. I was make up with my ex twice after serious break up.

(U can try your, I gonna guess.)

U will get answer in next updates..

⊠⊠⊠⊠⊠⊠⊠⊠⊠⊠⊠⊠⊠⊠

Adishh POV:

It's been a week since our fight, and we haven't talked since. I keep thinking about how she's supposed to fly out to Sweden in five days. The silence between us is just getting heavier. Every day that passes makes me more anxious, thinking this might be it—that she might actually leave for good this time. We've had our share of arguments before, but this feels different, like if we don't fix things now, we might never get another chance. I know I should probably call or something, but after how we left things, I'm not even sure she wants to hear from me. Every time I think about reaching out, I end up pacing around, worried she'll just shut me down. But then again, I miss her like crazy. The apartment feels so empty without her, and it's like every corner reminds me of her. I've got to do something, right? I mean, I can't just let her go without trying to make things right.

Yes my heart is just screaming to go and stop her from leaving for Sweden. But then, I keep replaying that moment in the hospital when she insulted me. It stings, you know? I mean, I believe in putting love above all, but then there's self-respect too, which I can't just toss aside. I'm really stuck here, wrestling with my feelings. Should I just let go of my pride and make things right, or should I stand my ground? It's a tough spot to be in, really.

Flashback:

I was buried in my thesis work in the empty dormitory of the hospital, trying to juggle reading and writing, when I heard footsteps approaching. Looking up, I saw Ankitha entering the room. "Hi Dr. Adishh," she greeted, taking a seat across from me.

I wasn't really in the mood for interruptions. "How did you know I was here?" I asked.

"I asked Trishul," she replied, casually placing her hands on my shoulders. Just then, Trishul walked in with Adhya. My spirits lifted at the sight of her, but Ankitha's intrusive behavior was grating on me. I managed a smile for Adhya, though she turned her face away, clearly upset. "Trishul, just hand over the thesis papers soon. I've got a ton of work on my plate," she said briskly.

"But it's lunch break, isn't it?" I pointed out, only to be met with silence.

As she made to leave, I reached out, catching her hand, pleading with my eyes for her to pause. She stopped, turning to face me.

"You guys fought again?" Trishul asked, looking between us.

"No, just an argument," I responded, trying to keep the peace.

"I wasn't arguing, Mr. Adishh," she snapped, her voice rising slightly.

I bristled at her tone. "Come again? What did you just call me?" My response was sharper than intended.

"Mr. Adishh," she repeated with a smirk.

"Okay, you seem completely prepared to leave and go forever," I retorted arrogantly.

"That was your fucking suggestion," she shouted back at me, anger flashing in her eyes.

"So, we can work on long-distance relationship?" I asked, trying to understand her perspective but struggling to keep my cool.

"Yeah, well, my so-called caring boyfriend decided he'd choose his career over our one-year relationship. That's how he convinced me to leave," she said, her voice flat and devoid of emotion, while I struggled to care less.

The confrontation escalated quickly, emotions running high. "Just drop all this drama!" I shouted, my patience fraying.

"I'm already on it. Goodbye then!" Adhya snapped back, her voice cold.

"Are you saying we're breaking up?" The words spilled out, tinged with disbelief and anger.

"Borking up? You are a fucking doctor not for romance." she mocked, her words cutting deep.

I had no interest in continuing this painful exchange, she turned to leave, but the weight of everything unsaid was suffocating. As I started to walk away, something inside me snapped. I reached out, trying to pull her back by the waist, desperate to resolve things. But instead of pulling her closer, she spun around and slapped me, the sound echoing down the empty hallway.

It was the first time anything like that had happened to me. I stood there, stunned, as she immediately muttered an apology. But it was too late; my anger surged beyond my control.

"We're done, Adhya!" I yelled, my voice breaking as I stormed away, tears blurring my vision. The echo of our harsh words and the sharp sting of her slap lingered, marking the bitter end of what we had..

My thoughts were shattered by the sound of the doorbell. When I opened the door, I couldn't believe my eyes—it was Adhya. My heart raced with a mix of anticipation and dread, wondering what she had to say.

I offered her a seat, but she remained silent, her expression unreadable.

"Our parents are coming on Tuesday, and I have a flight at 8 am on Wednesday. I don't want to burden them with the details of our breakup; they really blame me for this. Can you please keep quiet about it? I've managed to convince them that it's just a temporary separation, so please don't complicate things." Her words were steady, but I could sense the underlying turmoil in her voice.

I simply nodded in response, too stunned to form coherent words. "Do you have any questions about this?" she asked, her eyes searching mine. "And one more thing—could you please join us at the airport if you have the time?" With that, she turned and left, leaving me to grapple with the weight of her request and the ache in my heart.

I couldn't believe five days had flown by—I couldn't even remember how I spent them. It was 4 am, and I found myself at Adhya's PG along with her parents and Advish. They stayed with me last night, but Adhya refused to give a reason for her sudden departure. Despite my longing for her presence, nothing seemed to work.

Adhya arrived with a large trolley bag, a backpack, and a small carry bag. I helped her load them into the car, taking the driver's seat while uncle sat in the passenger seat. Adhya, aunty, and Advish settled in the back. Advish wasted no time teasing Adhya with my name, and she couldn't help but laugh along. Despite the early hour, the traffic was light, and we reached the airport quickly. I accompanied Adhya inside to help with the boarding pass procedure.

"Thank you for coming, or else everyone are doubted about our relationship status especially Advish. Answering him if will be big deal so act normal, I dont any mess at the end" she said gratefully.

"No need for thanks, I would have come even without an invitation, and this is not a end, I hope....." I replied casually but run out od words

"Sounds good, continue." she smiled softly.

"You're coming back after three months, right, laddu?" I asked, trying to keep the conversation light.

"I have no idea, Adishh," she replied, her tone somber. The use of my name pricked at my heart.

"You still have two hours before your flight, right?" I asked, trying to prolong our time together.

She just hummed.

Chapter 35

Okay.... I know i'm damn late this time I apologize. Sorry readers.

I have damn lazy and stuck with story cum personal reason. I will never repeat this again.

Your sincerely Sanvi.

Adhya's POV:

After all the procedures were done, my parents and Advish joined us, and Trishul arrived to say goodbye with a gift box. I hugged everyone, accepting their send-off gifts. When I reached Adi, I could sense the tears and apology in his eyes, but I thought it was too late. I knew I had overreacted, but his words, "I would have chosen career over you," had made me decide to let go of this relationship and move on to Sweden.

We had agreed not to tell our parents about our breakup, so I hugged him and broke into a pool of tears. I knew I was lying to myself; I missed him and would miss him every second. Moving on from this relationship was proving to be incredibly tough. Throughout the hug, I was waiting for him to say just one word, "Please stay," and I would have stayed with him forever. But it didn't happen as I had hoped. He broke our hug, placed a soft kiss on my forehead, and said, "I will miss you." I smiled through my tears and headed toward boarding.

The plane took off and left me all alone. I was unable to hold my tears any longer. I buried my face in my hands, tears flowing freely now. I thought about everything we'd been through—the good and the bad—and all of a sudden, I felt a pang in my heart. I knew I was making the right choice. At least, I told myself that. I didn't want to go through what we had just experienced. It was better this way, wasn't it?

I tried to convince myself that I wasn't lying to myself, but I wasn't entirely sure anymore. It hurt to be apart from him, but I had to do this for my career. If we stayed together, I would just end up holding him back. He deserved better than that, didn't he? I repeated this over and over again until I fell asleep.

The plane landed safely, and I collected my belongings from the overhead compartment. I felt a sudden wave of nerves wash over me, and I tried my best to ignore it. But as I walked to the exit, the nerves only intensified. What would people think if they found out I was leaving my hometown to move to a foreign country? Would they even care? After all, it wasn't like I had a big social life to speak of.

I landed in Sweden with a sense of anxiety, but at the same time, I was excited to start my new adventure. The airport was buzzing with activity, and everyone seemed to be in a hurry.

Author pov:

Adhya took a deep breath, clutching her suitcase as she stepped into the bustling terminal at Stockholm Arlanda Airport. The unfamiliar surroundings, the foreign language, and the crisp Scandinavian air all combined to create a sense of both excitement and apprehension. She reminded herself that this was a fresh start, a new chapter in her life.

As she navigated her way through the airport, following the signs to baggage claim, her mind kept drifting back to Adish. She could still see his face, the way his eyes had silently pleaded with her during their goodbye. The memory was bittersweet, a mixture of regret and resolve. She had to focus on her career now, no matter how much it hurt.

Back in their hometown, Adish stood by the window of his hospital office, staring out at the cityscape without really seeing it. The hospital was as busy as ever, patients and staff moving in a constant dance of care and urgency, but his thoughts were miles away. He had thrown himself into his work, trying to drown out the emptiness left by Adhya's departure. But no matter how hard he tried, her absence was a gnawing void he couldn't ignore.

Every corner of the hospital reminded him of her. The cafeteria where they used to have coffee during breaks, the garden where they sometimes sat and talked, even the sterile, impersonal hallways—they all echoed with memories of her laughter and her presence. He missed her terribly, the pain of their separation a constant, dull ache in his chest.

He found himself replaying their last moments together over and over. Her tear-filled eyes, the way she had clung to him, the unspoken words hanging in the air between them. He knew he had made a mistake, that his words had hurt her deeply. "I would have chosen career over you." The regret of that statement was like a weight on his soul. Why hadn't he asked her to stay? Why hadn't he fought for their love?

Adish sighed deeply, rubbing his tired eyes. He wished he could turn back time, take back those careless words, and show her how much she meant to him. But now she was gone, and he was left with nothing but memories and what-ifs.

Meanwhile, Adhya stepped out of the airport into the cool, fresh air of Stockholm. She hailed a cab and gave the driver the address of her new apartment. As the city unfolded around her, she tried to focus on the possibilities ahead. The new job, the new experiences, the new people she would meet. She had to make this work, for her sake and for Adish's. They both deserved to find their own paths, even if it meant those paths had diverged.

As the cab drove through the scenic streets, Adhya looked out at the city with a mix of wonder and trepidation. This was her new home now, a place where she could reinvent herself and chase her dreams. But as she settled into her seat, her thoughts inevitably drifted back to Adish. She couldn't help but wonder what he was doing, how he was coping with her absence.

In the quiet moments between her new life in Sweden and the bustling activity around her, she knew she would always carry a piece of him with her. And perhaps, in some distant future, their paths might cross again when they were both ready to take that first step back to each other.

Chapter 36

A dhya's POV:

Three months had passed since Adi and I broke up and since I moved to Sweden for my research associate position. Life had become a series of routines, immersed in work, and trying to ignore the constant ache of missing him. My colleagues were kind, and the research was fulfilling, but the void Adi left was impossible to fill.

Tonight, however, was different. My colleagues had organized a party to celebrate a successful project milestone. The atmosphere was lively, and laughter filled the room. I had dressed up for the occasion, trying to shake off the melancholy that had settled in my heart. The night was young, and for once, I wanted to forget my sorrows and enjoy the moment.

We were in the middle of a game of Truth or Dare when it happened. The bottle spun and landed on me. My friend, Clara, grinned mischievously.

"Truth or dare, Adhya?" she asked.

I sighed, deciding to go with the safer option. "Truth."

Clara's grin widened. "Tell us about your dating life. Any special someone?"

My heart skipped a beat. The memories of Adi flooded back, and I felt a lump form in my throat. Trying to maintain my composure, I took a deep breath.

"His name is Adishh," I said softly. "We were together for a year before I came here."

The room grew quiet as my friends listened intently. I could feel the weight of their curiosity and sympathy.

"What happened?" Clara asked gently.

I was about to explain when the door to the party room opened. My vision blurred for a moment, and I blinked, trying to focus. Standing there, looking just as handsome and heartbroken as I remembered, was Adi.

For a moment, time stood still. My heart raced, and I struggled to maintain a neutral expression. Adi's eyes met mine, and I could see the mix of emotions in his gaze—love, pain, longing.

He walked towards me, and I felt every step he took echo in my heart. My friends, sensing the tension, fell silent.

"Adhya," he said softly, his voice trembling.

"Adi," I replied, trying to keep my emotions in check.

Clara, ever the observant one, broke the silence. "So, this is the special someone?"

I nodded, unable to tear my eyes away from Adi. "Yes, this is Adishh."

Adi looked around, acknowledging the curious faces before focusing back on me ans whispered "so, i'm that special one." And winked at me.

My heart beat fasten at his words. The three months of separation, the countless nights of missing him, all came rushing back.

But I couldn't let my emotions overwhelm me, not now. I pulled him out for empty space where there is no one.

"I'm glad you're here, Adi," I said, my voice steady. "But why now?"

He stepped closer, his eyes never leaving mine. "Because I got call from someone a month before, they started cursing me.....

Flashback

Author pov:

Three months after their breakup, Adhya finds herself drunk and overwhelmed by her feelings for Adishh. She decides to call him, unable to hold back her emotions any longer.

Adhya: *slurring her words* "Adi, you...you absolute bastard. How could you just let me go like that?"

Adishh: *groggily answering the phone* "Adhya? Is that you? It's... it's late. Are you okay?"

Adhya: "No, I'm not okay! You fucking left me, and now I'm here alone in Sweden, missing you every damn day. You asshole!"

Adishh: *sighs* "Adhya, you're drunk. Maybe we should talk about this when you're sober."

Adhya: "Sober? Fuck sober! I need to say this now. Do you know how much it hurts to see your empty side of the bed every night? To go through the day without hearing your stupid voice?"

Adishh: *softly* "I miss you too, Adhya. Every single day."

Adhya: "Then why the fuck are we apart, huh? You said that career was more important than you. And saud Your will chose work over us. And did try to stop me airport if you said one word I would have stayed there forever, forever with you. I want you kill youn for that, But you know what? I...I still want you. I still need you.

Adishh: "Adhya, I was an idiot. I thought I was doing the right thing, but I've regretted it every day since."

Adhya: *voice dropping to a seductive whisper* "You know, Adi… you're my favorite sandwich. I want you to come over and eat me up, just like you used to."

Adishh: *breathing heavier* "Adhya, you're really drunk. You don't know what you're saying."

Adhya: "Oh, I know exactly what I'm saying. I miss the way you touched me, the way you made me feel. I miss your hands on my body, your lips on mine. God, I miss you so much it hurts."

Adishh: *voice thick with emotion* "I miss all of that too, Adhya. More than you can imagine."

Adhya: "Then why aren't you here? Why aren't you fucking here with me right now? I need you, Adi. I need you to make me feel whole again."

Adishh: "If I could, I'd be there in a heartbeat. But you're there, and I'm here… and it kills me."

Adhya: *moaning softly* "Remember how you used to make me beg for it? How you'd tease me until I couldn't take it anymore?"

Adishh: *groans softly* "Adhya, you're driving me crazy."

Adhya: "Good. I want you crazy. I want you to remember every inch of my body, every sound I made when you touched me. I want you to know that no one else could ever take your place."

Adishh: "Adhya, please… you're making this so hard."

Adhya: "I want to make it hard, Adi. I want you to come to me, to take me, to remind me of what we had. Because I can't stand being without you."

Adishh: *voice cracking* "I… I love you, Adhya. I never stopped. I was a fool to let you go."

Adhya: "Then come back to me. Come back and make me yours again."

Adishh: "I will, Adhya. I promise. I'll find a way to fix this, to be with you."

Adhya: "I'll be waiting. Just don't make me wait too long, okay?"

Adishh: "I won't. I swear."

As the call ends, Adhya feels a mix of relief and longing. She falls asleep with the phone still in her hand, a faint hope blossoming in her heart that maybe, just maybe, things will change.

Adhya's POV:

'Fuck man what I have done' I cursed myself how will I face him. With some amount confidence "all this are bullshit talk, I was drunk and with out of control, I have said something never mind."

"But I do." He bring his face to my face length. My stupid heart was out of control. By then Clara came here find us " Adhya, you can take Adishh home has I said before I will be out of station for month." I wished that earth should swallow me in a second.. I nodded at her and she felt.

"You can go back where you stay." I said him.

"I can but tonight jeevan girlfriend is join him, so....." He made a puppy face. Oh god this fellow is make crazy like hell.

"Okay you stay with me. I'll book cab wait." By saying I went inside and bid a bye for everyone and headed to home.

Chapter 37

Adhya's POV:

After the unexpected but heartfelt reunion with Adishh at the party, we said our goodbyes to everyone and caught a cab back to my flat. The ride was filled with a comfortable silence, both of us lost in our thoughts, savoring the renewed connection between us.

When we reached my flat, I offered Adi some water. "Make yourself at home. Get freshened up if you want," I suggested, trying to keep things casual despite the tension simmering between us.

He nodded and disappeared into the bathroom. I busied myself in the kitchen, trying to calm my racing heart. The sight of him after all these months, and the intensity of our conversation, had left me feeling a whirlwind of emotions.

A few minutes later, I heard the bathroom door open. I turned around, and my breath caught in my throat. Adishh stood there, half-naked, with just a towel wrapped around his waist. His damp hair clung to his forehead, droplets of water trailing down his well-defined chest. I couldn't help but stare, my jaw dropping slightly.

"Enjoying the view?" he teased, a playful glint in his eyes.

I quickly snapped out of my daze, feeling my cheeks heat up. "I... uh... didn't realize you didn't have spare clothes."

He stepped closer, a smirk playing on his lips. "Didn't think I'd need them. But I don't mind. If it makes you blush like that, I might just stay like this."

I rolled my eyes, trying to play it cool. "Very funny, Adi. Here, let me find something for you to wear."

I rummaged through my closet, finally pulling out an oversized unisex T-shirt and a pair of shorts. "These should do," I said, handing them to him.

He took the clothes but didn't make a move to change. Instead, he leaned against the doorway, his eyes never leaving mine. "You know, you look even more beautiful when you're flustered."

I crossed my arms, trying to maintain a semblance of control. "You're impossible."

"And you love it," he shot back, his voice low and teasing.

I felt a shiver run down my spine at his words. "Maybe," I admitted, trying to keep my voice steady.

He stepped closer, the towel slipping slightly, revealing more of his toned physique. "Just maybe?" he whispered, his breath warm against my ear.

I swallowed hard, feeling a mixture of desire and nervousness. "Adi, this is too much. Tell me, why are you here?" He went inside the room for dress cup, in no second he came back. With slower step he can near me and he gently cupped my face, his thumb brushing against my cheek. "Because I missed you. I want my Adhya back in my life."

His words sent a jolt of electricity through me. "Then why did you let me go?" I asked, lowering my eyes.

He removed his hand from my cheek. "Adhya, dreams are important, but I thought we had plenty of time."

"But for me, you're my dream. I dream about our future, that includes us, Adhya and Adishh, and also our kids. But your words brought insecurity in our relationship in a second. I can't handle all those, Adi," I said, tears forming in my eyes.

He leaned in, his lips just a breath away from mine. "I'm sorry," he murmured, closing the gap between us and kissed me.

I melted into his embrace, my hands finding their way to his chest, feeling the warmth of his skin under my fingertips. I didn't want to break our moment.

His hands roamed over my back, pulling me closer until there was no space left between us. I could feel the heat radiating from his body, the raw desire in his touch. When he finally pulled away, we were both breathless.

"Idiot, why did you kiss me?" I whispered, still catching my breath.

He chuckled softly, his eyes filled with affection and desire. "Because I love you," he replied, his voice husky.

I felt a blush creep up my neck. "Stupid, you're acting like a creep."

He smiled, gently caressing my cheek. "I have something to tell you, Adhya. can we just go for roof top."

I stared at him, shocked. "Why? What there—"

He interrupted me, taking my hand. "I know, but they believe in us, and so do I. Come with me, I want to show you something."

He led me to the rooftop, his hand warm and steady in mine. As we stepped out into the cool night air, my breath caught at the sight before me. The entire rooftop was transformed into a paradise, a blanket of flowers underfoot, their scent mingling with the crisp breeze. Soft lights twinkled around the edges, casting a romantic glow that made everything feel magical.

As I walked forward, I noticed a path of rose petals leading to the center of the rooftop. Each step I took was accompanied by the distant sound of fireworks preparing to ignite. My heart raced, anticipation and love swelling within me.

Adi guided me along the petal-strewn path, his presence calming yet electrifying. When we reached the center, I saw balloons slowly rising into the night sky. They were adorned with tiny lights, creating a trail of shimmering stars. As the balloons ascended, they revealed a message written in delicate script: "Will you marry me?"

Tears filled my eyes, blurring the vision of the beautiful scene. The fireworks erupted in the background, painting the sky with vibrant colors and patterns. It felt like the universe was celebrating this moment with us.

I turned to Adi, his face illuminated by the glow of the fireworks. His eyes, filled with love and vulnerability, met mine. He took a deep breath, his voice steady but laden with emotion.

"Adhya," he began, taking my hands in his. "I've made mistakes, and I've hurt you. But through it all, one thing has remained constant: my love for you. You are my dream, my everything. I don't want to spend another day without you by my side."

He got down on one knee, pulling out a small velvet box. Opening it, he revealed a stunning ring that sparkled even brighter than the fireworks.

"Will you marry me?" he asked, his voice breaking slightly with emotion.

My heart felt like it was about to burst with happiness. The reality of the moment, the genuine love in his eyes, and the thoughtfulness of the surprise made it feel like a dream. Tears streamed down my face, but they were tears of pure joy.

I nodded, without my knowledge

He slipped the ring onto my finger, and I pulled him up into a tight embrace. The world around us faded as he kissed my forehead, sealing the promise of our future together. The fireworks continued to light up the sky, but the real spark was the love between us, reignited and burning brighter than ever.

This moment, under the starlit sky, surrounded by flowers and fireworks, with Adi's heartfelt proposal, was something I would cherish forever. It was a beautiful, tangible expression of our love, one that had weathered storms and emerged stronger. And as we held each other, I knew that this was just the beginning of our new, beautiful chapter together.

Chapter 38

Adhya's POV:

After breaking the hug, I didn't say a word. I turned and started walking towards the elevator, my heart pounding. The rush of emotions from the proposal still tingled in my veins, but a part of me remained guarded.

Adi followed me silently, his presence a comforting shadow. We stepped into the elevator, and as the doors closed, the intimacy of the small space seemed to amplify the tension between us. Adi took a deep breath and broke the silence.

As the elevator doors closed and we began our descent, Adi broke the silence. "Adhya, there's something else I need to tell you," he said, his voice low and earnest. "Our parents are planning our wedding. That's why I came here to propose to you."

My heart, which had been soaring moments ago, felt a sudden jolt. I turned to him, my eyes narrowing. "Adi, are you serious? You came all this way to propose because our parents are planning our wedding?"

He swallowed hard, realizing his mistake. "I meant, I wanted to propose to you on my own terms, to show you how much I love you and want to spend the rest of my life with you."

I gave him a piercing glare, frustration bubbling up. "You should have led with that, Adi. You just know how to ruin the moment, don't you?".

Realization dawned on his face, and he looked genuinely remorseful. "I thought… I wanted to show you how serious I am, how much I love you," he stammered.

The elevator doors opened, and we walked into the flat. I needed to clear my head. "I'm ordering some food," I said curtly, pulling out my phone.

As I set up the table and arranged the dishes, I felt his presence behind me. He wrapped his arms around my waist, pulling me close. His lips found the nape of my neck, kissing softly, sending shivers down my spine.

"Adhya, please," he murmured between kisses. "I love you. I'm sorry for everything."

I took a deep breath, steadying my emotions. "Just because I agreed to marry you doesn't mean I've forgiven you," I said, my voice firm.

He stopped kissing me, confusion evident in his eyes as he turned me around to face him. "What do you mean?" he asked, his hands still holding me gently.

"It means," I began, looking straight into his eyes, "that I'm giving you a chance to prove yourself. You hurt me, Adi. You need to earn my trust back.

Adishh's POV:

I felt a lump in my throat as Adhya's words sank in. She was right. I had messed up, and now I had to make things right. I couldn't just expect everything to go back to the way it was.

"I'm sorry," I said, my voice filled with sincerity. "I know I hurt you, and I know it won't be easy to fix things. But I'm ready to do whatever it takes to make it right. I love you, Adhya. More than anything."

She looked at me, her eyes softening just a bit. "Prove it," she said simply, turning back to the table to finish setting up.

The food arrived, and we sat down to eat. The air was thick with unspoken words and unresolved emotions. I watched her, the way she moved, the way she avoided my gaze. I wanted to reach out, to bridge the gap between us, but I knew it would take time.

After dinner, as we cleaned up, I couldn't resist any longer. I walked up behind her, pulling her into my arms once again. This time, I kissed her with more intensity, my lips seeking hers with a desperate need.

"Adhya," I whispered against her lips, "I will do everything to earn your trust back. I won't let you down again."

She responded to my kiss, her lips softening against mine. The kiss deepened, a mix of passion and promise. Her hands moved to my chest, fingers tracing the lines of my muscles, sending a jolt of desire through me.

We broke apart, breathless. She looked at me, her eyes filled with a mix of emotions. "This doesn't mean everything is forgiven," she said, her voice a whisper.

"I know," I replied, holding her close. "But it's a start."

She nodded and continued "when are you going black?"

"Next week."

"I have one more question, how did you manage all this for my proposal?"

"I took jeevan and clara help." And I winked at her.

Adhya's POV:

After the intense conversation, I felt emotionally drained but also strangely at peace. We had taken the first step towards healing, and that meant a lot. The night was getting late, and I knew we needed to rest.

"You can sleep in my room tonight," I said, trying to sound casual. "I'll manage in Clara's room. She's not home."

Adishh immediately shook his head, his expression turning playful and childish. "No way, Adhya. I'm not letting you sleep in another room. We're sharing."

I sighed, knowing how stubborn he could be. "Fine," I relented, "but on one condition."

"Anything," he said eagerly, his eyes sparkling with mischief.

"You can't do any naughty or mischievous things," I warned, giving him a stern look.

He grinned, raising his hands in mock surrender. "Scout's honor. I'll be a perfect gentleman."

"Sure you will," I muttered, rolling my eyes.

We headed to my room, the familiarity of the space mixed with the strange new dynamic between us. I handed him a spare pillow and blanket. "Here you go. You can take the bed."

"And where will you sleep?" he asked, frowning.

"I'll just—" I started, but he cut me off.

"Nope. We're sharing the bed," he insisted, patting the mattress beside him.

I hesitated for a moment before crawling into bed next to him, keeping a cautious distance. "Remember, no funny business," I reminded him.

"I promise," he said, his voice soft and sincere.

Adishh's POV:

As we lay there in the dark, the reality of being so close to Adhya after all these months felt surreal. I wanted to hold her, to reassure her that I was here for the long haul. But I respected her boundaries.

We lay in silence for a few minutes, the only sound being our synchronized breathing. I couldn't help but sneak a glance at her. Her eyes were closed, but I could tell she was still awake.

"Adhya," I whispered, "thank you for giving me another chance."

She opened her eyes, her gaze meeting mine in the dim light. "I want to believe in us, Adi. I really do."

"You won't regret it," I promised, reaching out to gently squeeze her hand.

She gave a small, tired smile and closed her eyes again. "Goodnight, Adi."

"Goodnight, Adhya," I replied, feeling a warmth spread through me.

Adhya's POV:

As I drifted off to sleep, I felt a sense of cautious optimism. Sharing a bed with Adi felt both familiar and new. I was still guarded, but I couldn't deny the comfort his presence brought.

In the middle of the night, I woke up to find Adi's arm draped over me. I sighed, half-exasperated, half-amused. "Adi," I whispered, gently shaking him awake.

"Hmm?" he murmured, still half-asleep.

"Remember our deal?" I reminded him.

He chuckled softly, pulling me closer. "I'm not doing anything naughty, I promise."

I rolled my eyes but didn't push him away. Instead, I allowed myself to relax into his embrace, feeling a mix of exasperation and contentment.

"You're impossible," I muttered, but there was no real anger in my voice.

"And you love it," he replied, his voice drowsy and warm.

"Maybe," I conceded, snuggling a little closer. "Just don't push your luck."

He kissed the top of my head, and we both drifted back to sleep, the promise of a new beginning keeping us warm through the night.

Chapter 39

Adishh's POV:

I was in the car, heading towards the airport with Jeevan. The upcoming surgery next week loomed over me, but my mind was elsewhere. Adhya. Our recent moments together played on repeat in my head, and I couldn't shake off the worry that she might not come to see me off. Every mile closer to the airport felt like a mile further from her.

Jeevan noticed my distracted state and patted my shoulder. "She'll come, Adi. Just have faith."

I nodded, but the uncertainty gnawed at me. When we finally arrived at the airport, my eyes scanned the crowd anxiously as we made our way to the boarding gate. As the minutes ticked by, my hope dwindled.

Just as I was about to give up, I saw two figures running towards us. My heart leapt into my throat. It was Clara and Adhya, both out of breath but determined.

Adhya reached me first, slightly panting as she thrust a small bag into my hands. "I came here because I had something to give you for my parents. Make sure they get this," she said, her voice a mix of urgency and relief.

Clara caught up, laughing loudly. "For this stupid errand, you were crying and saying you were stuck in traffic?"

Adhya shot her a glare but couldn't help the small smile tugging at her lips. Clara hugged me tightly. "Take care, Adi. We'll miss you."

I turned back to Adhya, wiping a tear from her cheek. "I know you love me more than you admit," I said softly, looking into her eyes. "But I'll wait for you, no matter how long it takes."

Adhya smiled through her tears, her eyes reflecting a mix of emotions. "I'm not good at goodbyes," she whispered. "But I needed to see you one last time before you left."

I pulled her into a tight hug, feeling the warmth and softness of her body against mine. "This isn't goodbye, Adhya. It's just a see you later. I'll be back before you know it."

She nodded against my chest, and we stood there for a moment, savoring the closeness. Clara, ever the practical one, gently pulled us apart. "Alright, lovebirds. Time to board, Adi."

I gave Adhya one last kiss on the forehead, then turned to Jeevan. "Let's go."

As we walked towards the gate, I glanced back one last time. Adhya stood there with Clara, waving and trying to keep a brave face. My heart ached with the distance already, but her presence gave me the strength I needed.

The plane ride was filled with thoughts of her, the feel of her in my arms, and the promise of our future together. I knew that no matter the challenges ahead, I'd face them all for her. Because she was worth it. Every mile, every second apart, was worth it for the moment we'd be together again.

Adhya's POV:

The moment Adishh disappeared through the boarding gate, the tears I had been holding back finally spilled over. I couldn't stop them, no matter how hard I tried. The overwhelming sense of loss hit me like a tidal wave. I sat down on a nearby bench, my body shaking with sobs.

Clara, who had been by my side the whole time, looked genuinely worried. "Adhya, what's wrong? What happened?" she asked, her voice filled with concern.

I couldn't bring myself to speak. I just shook my head, burying my face in my hands. Clara sat down next to me, her arm around my shoulders, trying to comfort me. "It's okay, let it out," she said softly.

After what felt like an eternity, I finally managed to stop crying. I wiped my tears with a tissue Clara handed me, taking deep, shuddering breaths to calm myself. Clara watched me, her eyes filled with a mix of confusion and worry.

"Adhya, please tell me what's going on. You're freaking me out," she said, her voice tinged with frustration.

I took a deep breath, trying to compose myself. "I'm sorry, Clara. It's just... seeing Adishh leave was harder than I thought it would be."

She nodded, still looking puzzled. "But you knew he was leaving. Why are you so upset now?"

I shrugged, feeling embarrassed by my outburst. "I don't know. It just hit me all at once. The reality of him being gone, even if it's just for a little while."

Clara sighed, shaking her head. "You two are so dramatic. One minute you're crying your eyes out, and the next you're acting like everything's fine. You're giving me whiplash."

I couldn't help but laugh through my remaining tears. "I know, I'm a mess. But I'll be okay. I just needed to get it out of my system."

Clara smiled, relieved to see me lighten up a bit. "Good. Because you were seriously scaring me for a minute there. Let's get out of here, okay?"

I nodded, standing up and straightening my clothes. "Yeah, let's go. I don't want to stay here any longer."

As we made our way out of the airport, Clara continued to watch me closely, as if expecting another emotional breakdown at any moment. I felt a little guilty for worrying her, but I was grateful for her support.

In the cab ride home, Clara couldn't resist teasing me a bit. "So, are you going to be okay, or should I start carrying a supply of tissues with me at all times?"

I rolled my eyes, playfully nudging her. "Very funny. I'll be fine. Just needed to get that out of my system."

Clara laughed, the tension finally easing. "You two are like a soap opera. I swear, I never know what to expect with you and Adishh."

I smiled, feeling a bit more like myself. "Yeah, well, keeps life interesting, right?"

As we pulled up to our building, I felt a renewed sense of determination. Yes, saying goodbye to Adishh had been painful, but I knew we were strong enough to get through this. And with friends like Clara by my side, I knew I could handle whatever life threw my way.

Chapter 40

Adhya's POV:

It had been a month since I saw Adishh off at the airport, and now it was my turn to board a flight back home to India. I was filled with a mix of excitement and nervousness. After 15 days, Adishh and I were to be engaged, and preparations were in full swing at both our homes. Yet, there was an emptiness knowing that Adishh was still tied up with work at the hospital and wouldn't be back until just before the engagement.

My parents greeted me with a blend of joy and tears when I arrived. Being their only child, my homecoming after such a long time was a significant event. They had missed me terribly, and the house was buzzing with a whirlwind of activity and emotion.

"Welcome home, laddu" my mom said, wrapping me in a tight hug. I could feel her tears against my shoulder. "We missed you so much."

"I missed you too, Maa," I replied, hugging her back just as tightly.

Dad joined in, his usual stoic demeanor breaking as he pulled us both into a warm embrace. "It's good to have you back, my laddu muddu. The house feels complete again."

And most importantly all my favorite food was prepared from both in my home and Adishh mom, so we planned a family dinner unfortunately Adi missed it, but he joined us in video call with his vegetable salad. Advish looted all my imported things, And he started to call me attige(sister in law) and I love It.

As the days went by, the house was filled with relatives, friends, and endless discussions about the engagement. Amidst the preparations, my mother found a quiet moment to sit down with me.

"Laddu" she began, her voice soft but serious, "you know how important this is for us. You're our only child, and seeing you happy means everything to us. Are you sure about this? Are you happy with Adishh?"

I smiled, taking her hand in mine. "Maa, I love Adishh. I know we've had our ups and downs, but I believe in us. I believe in our love."

She nodded, her eyes glistening with unshed tears. "I just want to make sure you're truly happy. This is a big step, and we want the best for you."

"I am happy, Maa. And I promise, this is what I want."

One evening, as I was helping with the arranging for my engagement, my mom approached with my phone, it was from hospital that I should submit some important file so that I should go there.

I sighed with joy so i can see him, because on my boarding day he had a sudden emergency case so he missed it, i wont complaint about that because i know how is doctor life is, but missing him terribly. So I can finally meet him. "I caught up with work at the hospital, amma. So I should go for Bengaluru."

She nodded, So I'm going see adishh tomorrow.

Adishh's POV:

Back in Bangalore, life at the hospital was as demanding as ever. Surgeries, patient rounds, and late-night emergencies filled my days. Yet, despite the chaos, my thoughts constantly drifted to home, where preparations for our engagement were in full swing. I felt a pang of guilt for missing out on all the celebrations, but I knew this was necessary. Still, I couldn't help but feel a sense of longing.

However, amidst all the work and stress, there was a silver lining that kept me going: Adhya was coming to Bangalore. She had some work at the hospital here and would be staying with me for a few days. Just the thought of seeing her, holding her, and being close to her again filled me with excitement.

"Dr. Adishh, are you even listening?" Dr. voice snapped me back to reality.

"Sorry, doctor," I said, running a hand through my hair. He felt behind me and trishul.

"It's been a crazy few weeks."

Trishul chuckled, patting my back. "I get it, man. You have a lot going on. How's the engagement planning going?"

"Honestly, I feel terrible missing out on everything. But Adhya is coming here for a few days. That makes it a bit easier to bear," I admitted, a smile tugging at my lips.

Trishul raised an eyebrow, smirking. "Ah, so that's why you're on cloud nine. When does she arrive?"

"Tomorrow," I said, unable to hide my excitement. "She's got some work at the hospital here, so we'll get to spend some time together."

"That's great! You two deserve some time together, especially with everything that's been going on. Just make sure you make the most of it," trishul said with a knowing wink.

As the day went on, I found myself counting down the hours until Adhya's arrival. I finished my rounds, dealt with a few emergencies, and finally, it was time to head home. The thought of Adhya being there, waiting for me, filled me with a sense of anticipation and warmth.

The next day, I made sure everything was perfect for her arrival. I cleaned the apartment, made dinner reservations, and even picked up some flowers. I wanted to make sure she felt welcome and loved.

When I finally saw her at the Bus stop, my heart skipped a beat. She looked as beautiful as ever, her smile lighting up my world. I rushed to her, pulling her into a tight embrace, feeling the familiar warmth and comfort of her presence.

"Welcome home, love," I whispered into her hair, my heart swelling with happiness.

"It's good to be back," she replied, her voice soft and filled with emotion. "I've missed you so much." I said with naughty tone she glare at me.

We made our way to my apartment, and as soon as we stepped inside, I couldn't resist hugging her. It was a long hug, filled with all the longing and love we had for each other. When we finally pulled away, our eyes are fixed.

Adhya's POV:

Arriving in Bangalore felt like a dream. The anticipation of seeing Adishh again had kept me going through the long flight and the hectic weeks leading up to it. As soon as I saw him, all the stress and exhaustion melted away. His embrace was everything I needed and more.

"Welcome home, love," he whispered, his voice filled with emotion.

"It's good to be back," I replied, my heart swelling with happiness. "I've missed you so much."

The ride to his apartment was filled with comfortable silence, our hands intertwined, each of us savoring the moment. When we finally arrived, I was touched by how much effort he had put into making everything perfect. The clean apartment, the flowers, the dinner plans—it was all so thoughtful.

As soon as we stepped inside, he hugged me, a hug filled with love, affection and longing. It was as if we were making up for all the lost time and he's stand towards my words, OH MY MAN IS WALKING GREEN FLAG. but he should taste some ignoring medicine for my future.... Do I sound like a psycho, let it be a women can do anything for her love.

Chapter 41

dhya's POV:

After a perfect candlelight dinner arranged by Adishh in his apartment, we decided to take a walk. The night air was cool and refreshing as he led me to the 15th floor of his building. My curiosity piqued when he handed me a key.

"Open it," he said, a twinkle in his eye.

I turned the key and pushed the door open to reveal a beautifully decorated apartment. There was a sign that read, "I hope my queen likes her small palace." The room was filled with flowers and candles, and the view of the city from the floor-to-ceiling windows was breathtaking.

I turned to Adishh, my eyes wide with amazement. "This is... incredible," I whispered, my voice choked with emotion.

He smiled, taking my hand. "I wanted to give you a place where we can start fresh, Adhya. I've booked bus tickets for home to-morrow. After our engagement, we can come back and arrange everything according to your wish, like our dream house."

Overwhelmed with happiness, I threw my arms around him, holding him tight. "I love it. I love you," I said, my voice muffled against his chest. After sudden realisation "I mean this flat." He laughed at my stupid act.

We headed back to his apartment, but before we could enter, Adishh stopped me. He held my hands, his eyes serious yet filled with love. "Adhya, let's sleep together tonight."

I felt a flutter of nerves and confusion. "Adi, I…"

He gently cupped my face, his thumb brushing my cheek. "I miss my Adhya every day, in every moment. But I promise, I never crave just your body. All I need is you, my Adhya, the one I fell in love with. Let's just be together tonight, like we used to be."

His words melted my heart. The sincerity and depth of his love were clear in his eyes. I nodded, my emotions overwhelming me. "Okay, Adi."

As we entered the apartment, the air between us was charged with an unspoken understanding. We changed into comfortable clothes, and I found myself standing by the bed, feeling both nervous and excited.

Adi approached me, his hands resting gently on my shoulders. "Relax, Adhya," he murmured, his voice soothing but also in a teasing note. "I just want to hold you, to feel you close."

We slipped under the covers, his arms wrapping around me protectively. The warmth of his body against mine was comforting, and I felt a sense of peace that I hadn't experienced in months. He kissed my forehead, his breath warm against my skin.

"I love you, Adhya," he whispered. "More than anything in this world."

"Is it, Adi," I replied, but my man is still have that genuine smile. Oh my god. He pulled me closer to him.

As we lay there, holding each other, I realized that this was all I needed. The love, the connection, and the sense of belonging that we shared. It was perfect, just as it was.

The next morning, the sun's rays filtered through the curtains, casting a soft glow in the room. I woke up to the comforting weight of Adi's arm around me. For a moment, I just lay there, soaking in the warmth and the feeling of being so close to him.

"Good morning," he murmured, his voice still thick with sleep.

"Good morning," I replied, turning to face him.

He smiled, his eyes crinkling at the corners. "Did you sleep well?"

"Better than I have in months," I admitted. I dont want to spoil his mood cum my comfort too.

He pulled me closer, pressing a kiss to my temple. "I'm glad."

We stayed like that for a while, just enjoying the quiet intimacy of the moment. Eventually, though, we knew we had to get up and start the day. We had a bus to catch and a lot of things to prepare for our engagement.

After a quick breakfast, we packed our bags and headed to the bus station. The ride back home was filled with a mix of excitement and nervousness. I was looking forward to seeing my family and friendship because after 2days we are getting engaged and after 15days we getting married , but I was also anxious about the upcoming engagement and all the changes it would bring.

When we arrived, our parents greeted us with warm hugs and bright smiles. They were thrilled to see Adishh and me together, my parents love Adishh visa versa his parents love me much more than Adishh, it is best thing can ever get, and they couldn't stop talking about the engagement and all the preparations that were underway.

"Welcome home, Adhya," his mother said, her eyes shining with happiness.

"Thank you, Mom," I replied, hugging her tightly.

"And welcome to you, Adishh," my mother added, giving him a warm hug.

"Thank you, amma," he said, smiling.

My father clapped him on the back. "We're so happy to have you here, Adishh. You've been a part of this family for a long time, but now it's official."

Adishh smiled, his eyes flicking to mine. "I'm happy to be here, appa."

As the days went by, the house was filled with laughter, chatter, and the hustle and bustle of preparations. Adishh and I spent a lot of time with our family, this is benifit of marrying a neighbor, helping with the arrangements and catching up on everything we'd missed during our time apart.

The days flew by, and soon it was the night before our engagement. Our parents had arranged a small family gathering to celebrate. The house was filled with music, laughter, and the delicious aroma of homemade food.

As the evening went on, I found myself sitting with my mother, watching the festivities. She turned to me, her eyes filled with emotion.

"Laddu," she began, her voice soft, "you know you're our only child. Your father and I have always wanted the best for you."

I smiled, reaching out to hold her hand. "I know, amma. And you've given me everything I could ever ask for."

She sighed, her eyes glistening with unshed tears. "It's just... we're so happy for you, but also a little sad. You're all grown up now, and soon you'll have a family of your own."

I squeezed her hand, feeling a lump form in my throat. "Amma, I'll always be your daughter. No matter where life takes me, you'll always be my family."

She nodded, a tear finally escaping and rolling down her cheek. "I know, sweetheart. It's just hard to let go."

I hugged her tightly, feeling the warmth and love that had always been a constant in my life. "I'm not going anywhere, amma. I'm just adding more love to our family."

As we embraced, my father joined us, wrapping his arms around both of us. "We'll always be here for you, laddu," he said, his voice steady but filled with emotion.

"I know, appa. And I'm so grateful for that."

Chapter 42

Adhya's POV:

The day of our engagement had finally arrived. My family's home was a flurry of activity as relatives and friends gathered to celebrate. The rituals were carried out with precision, everyone's faces glowing with happiness and anticipation. I wore a beautiful traditional outfit, and Adishh looked dashing in his attire. The day was perfect, but the butterflies in my stomach wouldn't settle. There was an underlying excitement that wasn't just about the engagement itself.

Couple performances, family dances, and games had everyone laughing and enjoying themselves. Trishul and Advish, took charge of teasing the couples and coordinating the fun. I caught sight of Adi watching me with a smile on his face, and my heart fluttered. I felt a wave of excitement wash over me at the thought of marrying this amazing man.

Finally, it was time for the ceremony to begin. As I stood before him, I felt like my knees were going to give out from under me. But when our eyes met, the rest of the world faded away. I knew in that moment that I was meant to be with him. We were two people who found each other, and it was almost like fate had brought us together. As he gazed into my eyes, a soft smile appeared on his face. "Are you ready?" he asked, his voice soft and gentle. "I am," I replied, and we linked our hands as the ceremony began.

As the evening progressed, the dinner was served, and the photo session began. People gathered around, posing and capturing memories. Just as it was our turn, Adishh excused himself, saying he had an urgent call to attend to.

I watched him walk away, my heart pounding with anticipation. Just five minutes later, a roar of an engine filled the air. The guests turned towards the entrance, their eyes widening in surprise. A Himalayan bike, sleek and powerful, rolled into the venue, the rider clad in a leather jacket and helmet. The biker made a beeline towards me, extending his hand.

"Your chariot awaits, princess," he said, but I was shocked, confused. He pulled my hand and drag towards his bike, the bike's engine roaring once more. I looked over my shoulder.

As we rode off into the distance, I saw Adishh's father chasing after us. They he was stopped my Adish.

Advish's POV:

When they finally left the venue, I stepped forward to explain. "Plan executed well," I said with a grin for Trishul Anna.

My paapa, looked utterly confused. "What's going on here?" he asked, his voice a mix of anger and bewilderment.

I chuckled, trying to ease the tension. "It's on their bucket list, paapa. Adhya SIL always wanted to run away from her engagement with her boyfriend. And since her boyfriend and fiancé are the same person, we made it happen."

My father shook his head, exasperation clear on his face. "This is not the time for jokes, Advish. Look at her mother; she's worried sick."

I glanced at Adhya's mother, who did indeed look very concerned. I walked over to her, placing a reassuring hand on her shoulder. "Aunty, it was all planned. They're fine, see? They just needed a little adventure before settling down."

She looked from me to Adhya and back again, slowly starting to understand. "You kids and your crazy ideas," she muttered, but I could see the relief in her eyes.

Finally I inconvenienced everyone.... Uff being a younger one is so risky....

Adishh's POV:

As we rode through the city, the feeling of freedom and excitement surged through me. The streets were alive with the sounds and lights of the evening, but all I could focus on was Adhya, holding on to me tightly, her laughter ringing in my ears.

After a while, we stopped at a small ice cream parlor, one of her favorite spots. We ordered our favorite flavors and sat on the bench outside, savoring the sweet, cold treat.

"This is insane," Adhya said, her eyes sparkling with mischief. "I can't believe we actually did it."

I chuckled, taking her hand in mine. "It was the best idea you've ever come up with." She was clearly excited.

I nodded, a soft smile playing on her lips. "I do remember. But I didn't think we'd actually pull it off."

"Well, we did," I said, leaning in to kiss her gently. "And it's perfect. Just like this moment."

As we sat there, lost in each other, I felt a deep sense of contentment. This was what I had always wanted – to be with Adhya, to share these crazy, beautiful moments with her.

After finishing our ice cream, we took a slow ride back to the venue, enjoying the calm of the evening. As we approached, I could see the worried faces of our families, especially our parents. My father looked particularly concerned, while Adhya's mother seemed on the verge of tears.

Adhya's POV:

With everyone finally calming down and nice class for all four of us trishul was not exceptional it even I got soft hitting too, we rejoined the festivities. The guests had recovered from their initial shock and were now buzzing with excitement over our little escapade. It added an unexpected twist to the evening, something that would be remembered for years to come.

We danced to a slow song and he held me in his arms, my body pressed up against his. I loved the way he felt – strong and secure, but also soft and gentle. His eyes locked on mine, and I felt a wave of heat rush through me.

We danced together, a smile on his face as we moved slowly around the floor. "I'm so glad I found you," he whispered, leaning into my embrace.

"So am I," I replied softly, pressing his lips to my forehead.

Chapter 43

A dhya's POV:

The sun rose over the bustling city, casting a warm golden glow over everything it touched. Today was our wedding day. The culmination of our love story was finally here, and the house was alive with the sounds and scents of preparations for a traditional South Indian wedding.

I woke up early, the excitement and nervousness making it impossible to sleep any longer. My mother and aunts had already started bustling around, preparing the intricate decorations and the traditional breakfast of idlis, vadas, and coconut chutney. The aroma of jasmine flowers filled the air, mingling with the fragrance of incense and the distant strains of nadaswaram music, setting the perfect atmosphere for the auspicious day.

My bridal attire was a stunning Kanjeevaram saree, a deep maroon with intricate gold embroidery. It was a family heirloom, passed down through generations, and wearing it made me feel deeply connected to my heritage. My jewelry was equally traditional, with layers of gold necklaces, earrings, bangles, and a delicate maang tikka adorning my forehead. The final touch was the jasmine flowers weaved into my hair, their fragrance enveloping me in a comforting embrace.

As I sat down for my bridal makeup, my heart raced with anticipation. This was the moment I had dreamed of, and yet it felt surreal. My bridesmaids, a mix of cousins and close friends, fluttered around me, helping with the final touches and keeping my nerves at bay with their light-hearted banter.

"Ladhu, you look like a goddess," my cousin Meera said, her eyes shining with admiration.

"Thank you, Meera," I replied, smiling at her through the mirror. "I'm just so nervous. What if something goes wrong?"

"Nothing will go wrong," she assured me, squeezing my shoulder. "Today is your day, and everything will be perfect."

Adishh's POV:

Meanwhile, across town, I was experiencing my own whirlwind of emotions. The house was filled with the sounds of laughter and the clinking of breakfast dishes as my family prepared for the big day. My attire for the wedding was a traditional white veshti and angavastram, simple yet elegant, representing the purity of our union.

As I stood in front of the mirror, adjusting my attire, my best friend Trishul walked in, a mischievous grin on his face.

"Ready to take the plunge, buddy?" he asked, slapping me on the back.

I chuckled, though my hands were trembling slightly. "Ready as I'll ever be. I just hope Adhya is as excited as I am."

"She's probably as nervous as you are," he said, handing me a garland of fresh jasmine flowers to wear around my neck. "But today is the start of a new chapter for both of you. And it's going to be amazing."

His words were comforting, and I felt a renewed sense of determination. Today, I was marrying the love of my life, and nothing could overshadow that joy.

The Ceremony:

The wedding venue was a beautiful temple, adorned with vibrant decorations and surrounded by the lush greenery of its gardens. The entrance was lined with traditional kolams (rangoli) and oil lamps, creating an atmosphere of warmth and welcome. Friends and family filled the space, their colorful attire adding to the festive spirit.

As I made my way to the mandapam, the sacred space where the wedding rituals would take place, I felt a sense of calm wash over me. The nadaswaram music played in the background, and the priest began chanting the mantras, his voice resonating with the sacredness of the occasion.

Soon, it was time for Adhya to make her entrance. The sight of her took my breath away. She was radiant, a vision of grace and beauty. Her eyes met mine, and in that moment, all my nervousness melted away. This was where we were meant to be, together, forever.

Adhya's POV:

Walking towards the mandapam, I felt like I was floating. The rhythmic chanting of the priests, the music, and the presence of our loved ones created an aura of pure magic. When I saw Adishh standing there, looking at me with so much love and admiration, my heart swelled with emotion.

The wedding rituals began, each one steeped in tradition and symbolism. We exchanged garlands, symbolizing our acceptance of each other. As we sat down in front of the sacred fire, the priest guided us through the various rites – the tying of the kankanam (sacred thread) on our wrists, the pouring of sacred water, and the recitation of vows.

One of the most poignant moments was when Adishh tied the mangalsutra (sacred necklace) around my neck. The touch of the cool gold against my skin was a reminder of the sacred bond we were forming. As he tied the final knot, he looked into my eyes and whispered, "I love you, Adhya."

"I love you too, Adi," I replied, my voice trembling with emotion.

Adishh's POV:

The ceremony continued with the saptapadi – taking seven steps around the sacred fire, each step representing a vow we made to each other. With each step, I felt our bond deepening, our commitment to each other solidifying. The final step was a promise to be best friends and life partners, supporting and cherishing each other through all of life's ups and downs.

As we completed the rituals, the priest declared us husband and wife, and the crowd erupted in cheers and applause. I felt a surge of joy and pride as I looked at Adhya, now my wife. We were surrounded by love and blessings, and I knew that this was just the beginning of our incredible journey together.

The Celebration:

After the ceremony, it was time for the reception. The venue was transformed into a lively celebration with twinkling lights, beautiful floral arrangements, and a sumptuous feast. The air was filled with laughter, music, and the clinking of glasses as guests toasted to our happiness.

Our families had prepared a series of performances – dances, songs, and even a comedic skit that had everyone in stitches. Trishul and Advish, being the entertainers they were, led the charge, ensuring there was never a dull moment.

Adhya and I had our first dance as a married couple, swaying to a romantic melody. As we moved together, I whispered in her ear, "This is the beginning of our forever."

She smiled, her eyes shining with tears of happiness. "I couldn't have asked for a more perfect day, Adi. Thank you for making all my dreams come true."

Adhya's POV:

The night was magical, filled with moments that I would cherish forever. From the emotional speeches to the impromptu dances, it was a celebration of love, laughter, and the start of our new life together.

One of the highlights was the traditional South Indian feast, served on banana leaves. The array of dishes, from spicy curries to sweet desserts, was a testament to the richness of our culture. Adishh and I shared a meal, feeding each other bites of our favorite dishes, surrounded by our families and friends.

As the evening drew to a close, we made our way to the photo booth, where we took countless pictures, capturing the joy and excitement of the day. Each click of the camera was a reminder of the beautiful journey we were embarking on.

Finally, it was time for us to leave. Our families had prepared a traditional send-off, with blessings and heartfelt goodbyes. As we stepped out of the venue, hand in hand, I felt a sense of completion. We were no longer two individuals; we were a team, ready to face the world together.

Chapter 44

A dhya's POV:

The sendoff ceremony was emotional, a bittersweet farewell to the life I had known and the family who had nurtured me. The courtyard outside the wedding venue was adorned with lights and flowers, the remnants of a day filled with joy and celebration. Now, it was time to leave, and the air was thick with emotions.

My parents stood with me, their eyes glistening with tears. My mother, always the strong one, couldn't hold back her sobs as she hugged me tightly. "Ladhu, take care of yourself. Be happy," she whispered, her voice breaking.

"I will, Amma. I promise," I replied, my own tears mingling with hers.

My father, usually reserved, looked at me with a mixture of pride and sorrow. "You've grown into a wonderful woman, Adhya. We're so proud of you," he said, his voice trembling.

"Thank you, Appa. I love you both so much," I said, hugging him tightly.

As I turned to leave, my friends and relatives gathered around, offering their best wishes and blessings. Meera, my closest cousin, pulled me into a tight embrace. "I'm going to miss you so much, Adhya. But I know you're going to be so happy."

"I'll miss you too, Meera. Thank you for everything," I said, my voice choked with emotion.

Finally, it was time to go. Adishh stood by the car, waiting patiently. His presence was a comforting anchor amidst the sea of emotions. He took my hand, giving it a reassuring squeeze. "Ready to go, love?"

I nodded, though my heart was heavy. As we sat in the car, I glanced back one last time, seeing my parents and friends waving, their faces a mixture of joy and sadness.

Adishh's POV:

The car ride home was quiet, filled with a mixture of emotions. I glanced at Adhya, her face still wet with tears. I reached over and took her hand, giving it a gentle squeeze. "It's going to be okay, Adhya. We'll visit often, and they're just next door." I laughed like a fool.

She smiled weakly, appreciating the reassurance. "I know, Adi. It's just hard to leave them. You dont know all this who it feel."

As we reached our home, I saw our families waiting outside, ready to welcome us. Adhya's parents are also there, funny but truth we are neighbor. They had planned a light-hearted celebration to ease the transition, knowing how emotional the sendoff had been.

"Welcome home!" my mother exclaimed, pulling Adhya into a warm hug. "We're so happy to have you as part of our family."

"Thank you, maa" Adhya replied, her smile a bit brighter now.

My father, always the jokester, couldn't resist. "So, Adishh, how does it feel to finally bring Adhya home?"

I chuckled, wrapping my arm around Adhya. "It feels perfect, paapa. Like everything is finally falling into place."

Our friends and relatives had gathered as well, turning the homecoming into a mini celebration. There were jokes, laughter, and a few more tears, but this time they were tears of joy.

"Didn't expect to see you two back so soon," Trishul teased. "Thought you'd run off on a honeymoon already."

"Soon enough," I replied, winking at Adhya. "But for now, we're just happy to be home."

Adhya's POV:

Despite the sadness of the sendoff, being back at our home felt comforting. The familiar faces, the laughter, and the warmth of our families made the transition easier. As the evening progressed, the atmosphere became more relaxed, filled with love and joy.

Later that night, as the festivities wound down and everyone started to leave, Adishh and I found ourselves alone because they have planned a First night, so all other shifted to my home. We sat on the balcony, looking out at the quiet night.

"Today was a whirlwind, wasn't it?" I said, leaning into him.

"It was," he agreed, wrapping his arm around me. "But we made it through. And now, we have the rest of our lives to look forward to."

I looked up at him, feeling a surge of love and gratitude. "Thank you, Adi, for everything. For making today so special, and for always being there for me."

He smiled, leaning down to kiss my forehead. "Always, Adhya. You're my everything."

As we sat there, under the starlit sky, I felt a sense of peace settle over me. This was just the beginning of our journey, and I knew that with Adishh by my side, anything was possible.

Adishh's POV:

The night was calm and peaceful, a stark contrast to the whirlwind of emotions we had experienced throughout the day. Holding Adhya close, I felt a profound sense of contentment. We had navigated through the emotional farewell, and now we were embarking on a new chapter of our lives.

"Let's make a promise," I said, breaking the comfortable silence.

"What promise?" Adhya asked, looking up at me with curiosity.

"No matter what happens, we'll always communicate. We'll always be honest with each other and never let misunderstandings come between us."

She nodded, her eyes reflecting the sincerity of her words. "I promise, Adi. We'll face everything together. But I think you have forgotten that you have to still please for your mistake."

"Okay my lord... But what about first night laddu." I cannot judge his smile because it was like foolish Still flirty smile. So maintain silence.

"I know, we both are tired we can do that some other day right." He whispered in my ears. I shock my head that it. He laughed so hard. "My daredevil wife, is scared of her husband. I should celebrate it." By saying this he went out of the room. I was blushing so hard if I tried to justify my behavior I would have surly caught my blushing face. After 2 minute he came with some juice and snacks "lets watch some movie please." I nodded.

And so, surrounded by the love of our families and the warmth of our home, we took our first steps into our new life together, cherishing every moment and looking forward to the adventures that lay ahead.

Chapter 45

Adhya's POV:

Three days had passed in a blur of rituals, blessings, and family gatherings. The wedding had been a beautiful, exhausting affair, and as much as I cherished every moment, I was ready to settle into our new life together. It was time to head back to Bangalore, to our new apartment, and resume our work.

"Everything packed?" Adishh asked, peeking into the room.

"Almost," I replied, folding the last of our clothes. "I can't believe we're finally going to start our life together in Bangalore."

He smiled, coming over to help me. "Yeah, it's been a long time coming. But before anything else, I have my tasks laid out by my beautiful wife. Forgiveness is a big one, and I know I have to work hard on it."

I gave him a teasing smile. "You better. But I'm sure you'll manage."

As we finished packing, I couldn't help but feel a mixture of excitement and nervousness. Our new apartment awaited us, and with it, a new chapter in our lives. But there was also the reality of our demanding jobs. Adishh had two surgeries lined up this week, and I was returning to my duties at the hospital as well. Our work was about to get back into full swing, but this time as a married couple, not just dating.

Adishh's POV:

The drive to Bangalore was filled with easy conversation and shared anticipation. I glanced at Adhya, her face reflecting the same mix of emotions I felt. We were heading towards a new life, and I was determined to make it as perfect as possible for her, starting with earning her forgiveness for the mistakes I had made in the past.

Our new apartment was waiting for us, and I had a few surprises planned to make it special. But first, duty called. As soon as we arrived, I had to prepare for the upcoming surgeries. Being a doctor meant that sometimes personal life had to take a back seat, but I was ready to balance both.

When we finally reached our apartment, Adhya's eyes lit up. "It's beautiful, Adi, it just like same I told you." she said, taking in the space.

"I'm glad you like it. But remember, this is just the start. We'll make it our dream home together."

We spent the rest of the day unpacking and settling in. There was a sense of newness in everything, from the way we moved around the space to the little routines we began to establish.

Adhya's POV:

The next morning, reality hit as we both got ready for work. It felt strange yet comforting to go through our morning routines together. "I still can't believe we're married," I said, sipping my coffee.

"Me neither," Adishh replied, buttoning his shirt. "But I wouldn't have it any other way."

We drove to the hospital together, a new normal for us. Walking into the building, I felt a sense of pride and happiness. We were a team, both in our personal and professional lives.

As the day progressed, I was caught up in my duties, but my thoughts often drifted to Adishh. I knew he was busy with his surgeries, but it felt good knowing we were under the same roof, working towards the same goals.

Adishh's POV:

The surgeries went well, but I couldn't shake off the thought of Adhya. It was strange but comforting to think that she was just a few floors away. During a break, I texted her, "How's your day going, Mrs. Adishh?"

She replied quickly, "Busy, but good. How are your surgeries?"

"Went well. Can't wait to see you later."

The rest of the day flew by, and before I knew it, we were driving back home. As soon as we walked into the apartment, the exhaustion of the day hit us both. But there was also a sense of accomplishment, of having faced the day together.

"Dinner?" I asked, pulling her into a hug.

"Sounds perfect," she replied, leaning into me.

We cooked together, a simple meal that felt special because we were doing it as a team. As we ate, we talked about our day, our plans, and the future. The conversation flowed easily, filled with laughter and shared dreams.

Adhya's POV:

After dinner, we settled on the couch, a comfortable silence enveloping us. I looked at Adishh, feeling a wave of gratitude and love. "You know, this feels perfect," I said, snuggling closer to him.

"It does," he agreed, kissing my forehead. "But remember, I still have to earn your forgiveness."

I smiled, knowing he was sincere. "You're on the right track."

As the night wore on, we talked about everything and nothing, enjoying the simple pleasure of being together. It was the start of our new life, and despite the challenges ahead, I felt confident that we would face them together.

Adishh's POV:

Holding Adhya close, I felt a deep sense of contentment. This was just the beginning, and I was ready for whatever the future held. With her by my side, I knew we could handle anything.

"Ready to call it a night?" I asked, feeling the day's exhaustion catching up with me.

"Yeah, let's get some rest," she replied, standing up and stretching.

We headed to our bedroom, the place where we would start and end our days together. As we lay down, I held her close, feeling grateful for this new beginning.

"Goodnight, Adhya," I whispered.

"Goodnight, Adishh," she replied, her voice filled with warmth and love.

And as we drifted off to sleep, I knew that no matter what, we would face it all together, as husband and wife.

Chapter 46

Adhya's POV:

Everything was going as usual. The novelty of being married was still fresh, but there was a comforting familiarity in our routines. After all, we had dated for a long time and used to be neighbors, so we had spent countless days together. But one evening, things took a turn.

It started with a simple plan. Adishh had promised to take me out to dinner, a chance for us to reconnect after a busy week. I had looked forward to it all day, imagining the warmth of his hand in mine, the soft glow of the restaurant lights, the intimate conversations that would flow between us.

But as the evening approached, I received a message from him: "Working late. Let's reschedule dinner." My heart sank. I felt disappointed, but I decided to be understanding. After all, work was important.

Hours passed, and I busied myself with a book, trying to keep my mind off the disappointment. When I finally heard the door open, it was much later than I had expected. I got up, ready to greet him, but stopped in my tracks as I saw the look on his face.

"Hey," I said softly.

"Hey," he replied, his voice distant.

"Did you have a long day?" I asked, trying to keep the conversation light.

"Yeah, something like that," he said, walking past me to the bedroom.

It wasn't until later, when I checked social media, that I saw the photos. Adishh was out to dinner, not working late as he had said, but with his colleagues. He hadn't even informed me. My disappointment turned to anger. How could he forget about our plans and not even bother to tell me?

When he finally emerged from the bedroom, I couldn't hold back any longer. "You lied to me," I said, my voice shaking with anger.

"What?" He looked genuinely confused.

"You said you were working late, but you were out with your colleagues. You forgot about our dinner plans, Adi."

He sighed, rubbing his temples. "I'm sorry, Adhya. It was a last-minute thing. I didn't mean to forget."

"But you did forget," I snapped. "And you didn't even bother to tell me. Do you know how that makes me feel?"

"Look, I said I'm sorry. Can we just drop it?"

"No, we can't just drop it. This isn't the first time you've done this. I need to know that I matter to you."

"You do matter to me," he said, his voice rising. "But I have responsibilities, too. I can't always put you first."

"That's not the point," I said, tears welling up in my eyes. "I just wanted you to consider my feelings. Is that too much to ask?"

He didn't respond, and the silence stretched between us. Finally, he turned and walked out of the room, heading to the guest bedroom. "Fine. I'll sleep in the other room tonight."

Adishh's POV:

The next morning, the tension was palpable. We barely spoke to each other, moving through our routines in silence. I felt a knot of guilt in my stomach, but I was also offended by how she had reacted. Couldn't she understand that sometimes things came up unexpectedly?

At work, I couldn't concentrate. My mind kept drifting back to our fight. I hated this silence between us, this cold wall that had sprung up overnight. I wanted to fix things, but I wasn't sure how.

When I got home that Even ring , the atmosphere was still icy. Adhya was in the kitchen, her movements precise and deliberate. She didn't look up when I entered.

"Adhya," I said softly, trying to break the silence.

She didn't respond, her back to me as she continued chopping vegetables. I walked over and gently placed my hand on her shoulder. "I'm sorry about last night. I should have told you about the change in plans."

She finally turned to face me, her eyes red-rimmed. "It's not just about last night, Adi. It's about feeling like I'm not a priority."

"You are a priority," I said, my voice earnest. "I just... I screwed up. I'm sorry."

Her shoulders sagged, and she let out a deep sigh. "I'm just tired, Adi. Tired of feeling like I'm always second to your work. Tired of you putting me on the back burner, even if it was unintentional. And I don't know what to do about it."

"Always same, I'm a doctor and you know how is a doctor life is. I want to take care of you, not make you sad. I think I will understand and respect my career." I said, reaching to hold her hand.

"Yes, and I should understand you too but what about my needs? What if I feel lonely and I want you by my side. I need your touch and love."

"I dont like drag much adhya, I have operation tomorrow, I dont like mess my mood with something like this."

"Okay, I will not disturb you." She said, with a defeated tone.

And next i found note that breakfast is ready and she us getting so she took a cab for hospital.

I felt a sharp pang in my chest, my stomach churning with unease. Was this it? Was this the beginning of the end?And even I left for hospital there was no energy to fight with her. All long day was busy, Trishul and me were heading towards canteen where I met Adhya after long time. She looked tired and upset. I stood near her with tray and a tea, trying to say something. She started to walk towards her table and I followed her.

She sat down, and I stood in front of her. "Adhya, what's wrong?" I asked, my tone soft.

"Just leave me alone, Adi. I don't want to talk." By saying this she left canteen, her ignorance drive me crazy.

Chapter 47

Adishh's POV.

It had been a long, grueling day at the hospital. Two major surgeries back-to-back had drained me, both physically and emotionally. As I drove home, my mind wandered back to the night before. I had promised Adhya a dinner date, but got caught up with colleagues and completely forgot to inform her. She had every right to be angry, and I felt like an absolute idiot for neglecting her like that.

When I finally walked into our apartment, I heard Adhya's voice from the living room. She was on the phone, and her tone was serious. I paused, trying to catch snippets of the conversation. Words like "law" and "legal action" stood out, sending a chill down my spine.

"I'm done with all this gouri, but still worried about court rules." she said to the person on the other end of the line.

My heart dropped, and I slowly crept forward, trying to listen to the rest of her conversation.

"I know," she sighed, running a hand over her face. "I just need a few more days. My case is almost ready, but I've got to meet the lawyer and work out some legal issues. If everything goes well, we can start the court proceeding within a few months."

My heart pounded as I connected the dots. Was she talking about divorce? Had I pushed her too far?

I couldn't bear the thought. In a state of panic, I rushed towards her and wrapped my arms around her from behind, holding her tightly. Tears streamed down my face as I buried my head in her shoulder, my emotions spilling out uncontrollably.

"I'm so sorry, Adhya," I sobbed. "I will never, ever avoid you again. Please, don't leave me."

She stiffened in my arms, clearly surprised by my sudden outburst. She quickly ended the call and turned to face me, her hands gently cupping my face. "Adi, what are you talking about?"

I looked at her, my vision blurred by tears. "I heard you talking about legal action and... I thought... I thought you wanted a divorce." I said sobbing heavily.

She let out a shaky laugh, wiping my tears with her thumb. "Adi, I was talking about our project patent, not divorce. I would never, ever divorce you."

I blinked, my tears slowing. "The project patent?" I asked, my voice a whisper. She smiled and nodded. "Yes, the project patent."

"But why were you talking about court, lawyer?"

She chuckled and placed her hand on my chest "then how will you register your patents if you don't do it in court."

She laughed and kissed my cheek "I can't believe you thought I was planning to divorce you."

I felt a mix of relief and embarrassment. "I'm such an idiot."

She chuckled, brushing my hair back. "Yes, you are. But you're my idiot."

I smiled and pulled her close, kissing her softly. I loved this woman more than anything else in the world, and I wasn't planning to lose her ever again.

"I'm hungry," she said after a while, gently nudging me away. "I'm going to get dinner ready, okay?"

I nodded, taking a seat on the couch. She turned to leave, then stopped. "And Adi?" I looked up at her. "Yes, laddu."

"I think your forgiveness is granted."

She kissed me on the lips before walking into the kitchen, leaving me alone with my thoughts.

"How could I forget about that?" I mumbled to myself, laughing at the ridiculousness of it all.

She said "lets set candle light dinner tonight." From the kitchen.

I got up from couch and walked towards kitchen. "Yes for sure sweetheart."

I laughed and hugged her from behind, kissing her cheek. We cooked food together and set the table ready. She went inside to get ready.

She came out with red hot saree, free hair, minimal jewellery oh my god she is so beautiful and hot. I went near her slide my hand in her bare waist kissed her softly. "Lets have food now like a starter my main course and dessert will be you." I said to her and she blushed.

We sat down and started to eat, everything was going so well. And she looked so happy. After some time she stopped eating and looked at me. "Lets dance a little."

She got up and stood near the stereo and pressed play. A romantic song started to play.

I got up and walked towards her and she held my hand and we started to dance.

"You look very beautiful and amazing tonight." I said to her. "Can I kiss you.?" I asked her. She nodded and we kissed, I broke the kiss "what If I couldn't control my kiss, we moved ahead." I felt that I'm flirt with my wife, still its her body her wish I should look after her concern first.

She smiled and pressed her body against mine and we continued to dance. I held her close, swaying gently from side to side, lost in the music. I could feel the heat of her body against mine, and I couldn't resist the urge to run my fingers through her hair. We slowly moved towards bedroom and command alex to stop the music, we just stared at each other for a moment before kissing each other hungrily.

"Sorry, I couldn't stop this time." I said and we both started to laugh. She then whispered in my ear "I like this." I pulled her close, resting my forehead against hers as she closed her eyes.

I stared into her eyes, the passion and love I felt for her, making my breath catch in my throat. Her beauty captivated me, and I felt myself growing harder. I wanted to take her right then, to show her how much I loved her and how much I needed her. But I held back, trying to control my urges.

I run my hand around her waist and slowly removed her saree pleats, exposing her half naked body. She looked up at me, her cheeks flushed with excitement. I leaned down, pressing my lips against her skin. My hands slid down her body, touching every inch of her soft, warm flesh.

She moaned softly, her hands gripping the sheets as I began to kiss her neck. I moved down to her collarbone and lower, kissing her chest. She gasped, and I felt her trembling in my arms. "Adi..." she whimpered, but I ignored her.

I continue to kiss her, slowly moving down to her breasts. I took one in my hand, squeezing it gently. She moaned, squirming against me.

I could see how wet she was, and it only made me harder. I felt a hunger rising within me, a desire to pleasure her as she had never been pleasured before. I moved lower, kissing her stomach. I reached her panties and gently pulled them off, revealing her naked form.

I kneeled down before her and spread her legs, revealing her dripping wet pussy. I smiled at the sight, admiring her body.

She is a goddess in human form. She is perfect in every way imaginable. I am truly blessed to have such a beautiful wife.

"You are perfect, my love." I whispered, leaning in to kiss her thigh.

"Please..." she moaned, but I ignored her, continuing my kisses.

I kissed her inner thighs, working my way up to her pussy. Her juices were dripping, and I could tell how excited she was.

I finally moved my lips over her pussy and began licking her slowly. She moaned loudly, her body trembling. I could taste her sweet juices, and I could tell she was close.

I licked her harder, focusing on her clit. Her moans became louder, and she thrust her hips against my face. She was close to orgasm, and I was determined to make her come.

I sucked her clit hard, causing her to cry out. "Adi!"

Now its time to set my dick inside her pussy. I move up, aligning my cock with her pussy entrance. "You ready?" I asked. She nodded.

I thrust myself deep into her, filling her up completely. She gasped, her body trembling from pleasure.

I began to move slowly at first, but soon I was fucking her hard and fast, plunging my cock deep into her pussy.

It felt incredible to be inside of her, to be connected like this. I could feel her tight pussy clenching around me, and it only drove me to go deeper.

I wanted to cum, to fill her with my seed, to claim her as my own. She cried out, her fingernails digging into my back as she climaxed.

I fucked her harder, wanting to give her more pleasure than she could ever experience. Her orgasm seemed to last for hours, her pussy quivering against my cock as she came.

Finally, I pulled out and came all over her stomach. My cum covered her breasts and belly. I collapsed on the bed, gasping for air.

She curled up beside me, and I held her close. "That was amazing, Adi."

"I'm glad you enjoyed it, love." I said, kissing her forehead.

We lay there in silence, enjoying the moment. I could feel myself beginning to fall asleep, but I didn't want to move. I wanted to stay right where I was, forever.

I let out a long breath, feeling tired. "I love you, Adhya."

"I love you too, Adi."

We lay in bed together, her head on my chest.

Adhya's pov.

Sun rays filtered through the curtains, filling the room with light. My head was resting on Adi's chest and our bare body was perfectly hugged in each other's arms. His muscular torso was smooth and warm, his body providing me comfort as we lay together in bed.

I felt him stir, his arms tightening around my waist. I felt shy but we are married, butterflies in my stomach. Actually he have a long eyelashes, I touched it then his sharp nose. I was amazed how handsome he was. Then I about touch his lips "I know you are awake, don't hide from me." I said.

He slowly opened his eyes and looked at me, his lips curled into a smile. "Morning my love." He said, his voice low and husky with sleep.

I tried to move my body, I felt little pain so I try not move too much. "Ouch" I said to him.

He noticed that so he moved me in bed slowly. "Are you okay?" He asked, his expression full of worry. I smiled foolishly, he got to know that it all about yesterday night effect "you know how to seduces your husband but you dont know handle the outcome of the results." He said, with a cheeky grin.

I blushed and looked away from him. He laughed softly and kissed me on the lips. His hand slid under my top and his warm hand caressed my breast. "Apply for leave today and rest your body." He said to me.

I nodded in response. "Do you want breakfast?" I asked him.

"Yeah, sure but I order something." He said, giving me a kiss.

Chapter 48

A dishh's POV

 Its been 1.5 years of our marriage, everything is as usual little fight, more love and sex. I have legal rights guys she is my wife, my love and vise versa.

It had been a regular, hectic day at the hospital, a blur of patient rounds and surgeries. My mind was preoccupied with the usual concerns of my profession when my phone buzzed in my pocket. Glancing at the screen, I saw it was a call from Adhya's junior, Gouri. My heart skipped a beat, sensing something was wrong.

"Dr. Adishh, Adhya fainted in the lab," Gouri's voice trembled on the other end. Without another thought, I sprinted towards the lab, my heart pounding in my chest.

When I reached, they had already shifted Adhya to another ward for testing. Anxiety clawed at my insides as I raced down the corridors, my thoughts a chaotic mess. Finally, I found her in a private room, lying on a bed, her face pale and streaked with tears. My heart broke at the sight.

"Adhya!" I rushed to her side, wiping away her tears and pulling her into a gentle embrace. "What happened? Are you hurt?"

She continued to cry, her sobs wracking her body. I held her tighter, my own fears mounting. "Adhya, please, talk to me."

Just then, the doctor walked in, a warm smile on her face. "Dr. Adishh, congratulations. You're going to be a father."

Her words didn't register at first, my mind still too busy with thoughts of Adhya. But when I finally understood what she'd said, I pulled her close, a mixture of elation and overwhelming relief. After a moment, the world stood still. I stared at the doctor, then back at Adhya, who was now crying even harder. The doctor shook her head and quietly left the room, leaving us alone.

I lifted Adhya's tear-streaked face, searching her eyes for answers. "So, you were asking about children, weren't you?" she asked with a crying face, her cheeks flushed. "You didn't seem interested in having any, so..."

Adhya took a shaky breath, her hands clutching mine tightly. "Adi, I didn't expect this. We always talked about planning for the right time, and I thought we still had time."

I stared at her in disbelief, the reality of the situation slowly sinking in. "So, it's true? I'm going to be a father?"

She nodded, tears spilling down her cheeks. "But you said that your not ready for baby, but..." she stuttered.

I pressed my lips to hers, drowning out her words with a deep, passionate kiss. "It's okay, love. I'm happy. Really. Adhya, I've always wanted to have a baby. But you matter to me more. It's your decision, I thought you said what you did because our parents asked about a baby when we visited them."

"No, no, no, you know what I mean, you know what I mean. I was scared because we always talked about it but you said you don't want to have baby soon, so I thought..." she rambled.

I smiled, my heart swelling with love for her. "Look, I'm going to be a father, and it's the best feeling in the world. I've always wanted children, but I wasn't sure if you did too. I didn't want to pressure you into something that might make you uncomfortable."

"But now you're happy?"

I smiled broadly, my eyes brimming with tears. "I'm very happy."

I felt Adhya tense up, and she looked down at her belly. "We're really going to do this, right? Have a baby together?"

I laughed and nodded. "Yes, love. I don't know how or when, but we'll do it together. I love you."

"I love you too, Adi," she whispered.

She gave me a shy smile, and I pulled her closer, pressing my lips against her forehead.

I was beyond happy. I couldn't believe my baby is inside her belly. My wife is pregnant, and it's because of me. I'm so lucky to have her.

We both went for the lab for an ultrasound and confirmed that we're going to have a baby. I felt overwhelmed and wanted to share this news with my parents as well, so they booked a ticket. We are going to spend the next week with them at our home.

They were delighted to hear that we're going to have a baby.

Adhya's POV

The day had started like any other, busy with my research and lab work. But suddenly, I felt dizzy, and everything went black. When I came to, I found myself in a hospital bed, surrounded by worried faces. The fear and confusion were overwhelming, and I couldn't stop the tears from flowing.

When Adi arrived, I could see the panic in his eyes. His touch was comforting, but I couldn't find the words to explain what I was feeling. It wasn't until the doctor congratulated him that the reality hit me hard – I was pregnant. The news brought a rush of emotions, leaving me even more overwhelmed.

"Adi, I didn't expect this. We always talked about planning for the right time, and I thought we still had time," I managed to say through my tears.

His laugh was unexpected, a sound that brought warmth to my heart. "Adhya, I've always wanted to have a baby. But you matter to me more. It's your decision, I thought you said what you did because our parents asked about a baby when we visited them."

I looked into his eyes, seeing the love and support shining there. "Adi, I... I was just scared. Scared of the responsibility, of how it would change our lives. But if you want this, if you believe we can do this, then... maybe I can believe it too."

He hugged me tightly, his warmth and strength enveloping me. "We can do this, Adhya. Together. We'll figure it out, like we always do. You're not alone in this."

Adishh's POV

I held her close, feeling her body slowly relax against mine. "Adhya, we're a team. We've always been a team. This baby will be a part of our team too. I promise, we'll make this work."

Her sobs subsided, replaced by a quiet sniffle. She pulled back slightly, looking at me with a mixture of hope and uncertainty. "But what about our careers, Adi? What about all our plans?"

I smiled, brushing a stray lock of hair from her face. "Plans change. We'll adapt. We'll find a way to balance everything. And our careers? We have each other's backs. We'll support each other, just like we always have."

A small smile tugged at her lips, the first hint of hope returning to her eyes. "You really think we can do this?"

I nodded, my heart swelling with love for her. "I know we can. And besides, we're going to have the cutest, smartest baby ever."

She laughed, a sound that filled the room with warmth and joy. "Okay, Adi. We'll do this. Together."

We sat there, holding each other, the weight of the news slowly lifting. The future suddenly seemed brighter, filled with new possibilities and challenges. But with Adhya by my side, I knew we could face anything.

Adhya's POV

As the initial shock wore off, I found myself beginning to feel a strange mix of excitement and anticipation. The idea of becoming parents, of bringing a new life into the world, was both daunting and exhilarating.

"Adi," I whispered, my voice trembling slightly. "I'm scared, but I'm also… excited. I can't believe we're going to be parents."

He smiled, his eyes twinkling with happiness. "Me too, Adhya. It's a big change, but it's also an incredible adventure. And I can't think of anyone else I'd rather share it with."

I leaned in, kissing him softly. "Thank you for always being my rock, Adi. I love you so much."

He kissed me back, his lips warm and reassuring. "I love you too, Adhya. More than anything in this world. And I promise, we'll make this work. Together."

As we sat there, holding each other, the future seemed less frightening and more filled with hope. We had each other, and soon, we'd have a new addition to our little family. And no matter what challenges lay ahead, we knew we could face them together.

The road ahead might be uncertain, but with Adi by my side, I felt ready to take the first step into this new chapter of our lives.

Together, we would build a future filled with love, laughter, and the joy of raising our child.

Adishh's POV

The days following the news of Adhya's pregnancy were a whirlwind of emotions and adjustments. We found ourselves navigating a new normal, one that included doctor's appointments, planning for the future, and countless conversations about our hopes and fears.

Every morning, I'd wake up earlier to make breakfast for Adhya, ensuring she ate well before heading to work. Her health and well-being became my top priority. We'd sit together at the kitchen table, sharing quiet moments before the chaos of the day began.

One evening, after a particularly long day at the hospital, I came home to find Adhya curled up on the couch, reading a pregnancy book. She looked up as I entered, a tired but content smile on her face.

"Hey," she greeted, putting the book aside. "How was your day?"

I sighed, kicking off my shoes and joining her on the couch. "Exhausting, but seeing you makes it all worth it."

She leaned into me, her head resting on my shoulder. "I'm glad you're home. I missed you."

I wrapped my arm around her, pulling her closer. "I missed you too. How are you feeling?"

"Better," she admitted, a hint of a smile playing on her lips. "It's still surreal, you know? Thinking about the little one growing inside me."

I placed my hand gently on her belly, feeling a surge of love and protectiveness. "I can't wait to meet them."

Adhya's POV

As the days turned into weeks, I found myself adjusting to the idea of being pregnant. It was a rollercoaster of emotions, but having Adi by my side made all the difference. His unwavering support and love gave me the strength to embrace this unexpected journey.

One night, as we lay in bed, I turned to him, feeling a mixture of excitement and nervousness. "Adi, I've been thinking... we should start preparing for the baby. Maybe start setting up the nursery?"

He smiled, his eyes filled with warmth. "Absolutely. Let's do it this weekend. We'll go shopping and pick out everything we need."

His enthusiasm was infectious, and I couldn't help but feel a surge of excitement. "Thank you for being so amazing, Adi. I don't know what I'd do without you."

He kissed my forehead, his lips lingering. "We're in this together, Adhya. Always."

Adishh's POV

The weekend arrived, and we found ourselves at a baby store, surrounded by cribs, strollers, and tiny clothes. Adhya's eyes sparkled with excitement as she examined each item, and I couldn't help but feel a sense of awe at the thought of becoming parents.

"Look at this crib, Adi," she said, pointing to a beautifully crafted wooden crib. "It's perfect."

I nodded, imagining our little one sleeping peacefully in it. "It's beautiful. Let's get it."

We spent hours in the store, selecting everything we needed for the nursery. It was a day filled with laughter, love, and a growing sense of anticipation for the future.

Back at home, we set up the nursery together. As we worked, I couldn't help but feel overwhelmed by the enormity of what lay ahead. But with Adhya by my side, I knew we could handle anything.

Adhya's POV

As the weeks turned into months, my pregnancy progressed smoothly. Adi was my rock, supporting me every step of the way. He attended every doctor's appointment, held my hand during the ultrasounds, and was there for me through every high and low.

One evening, as we sat on the couch, Adi resting his hand on my growing belly, I felt a tiny flutter. My eyes widened, and I looked at him, my heart racing.

"Adi, did you feel that?" I whispered, tears of joy filling my eyes.

He looked at me, his expression one of pure wonder. "Yes, I did. It's our baby."

We sat there, feeling the baby's movements, tears streaming down our faces. It was a moment of pure magic, one that brought us even closer together.

Adishh's POV

As the due date approached, I found myself filled with a mix of excitement and anxiety. I wanted everything to be perfect for Adhya and our baby. I took time off from work, wanting to be there for every moment of this incredible journey.

One night, as we lay in bed, Adhya turned to me, her eyes filled with love. "Adi, I know you're nervous, but we're going to be okay. You're going to be an amazing father."

Her words filled me with a sense of calm and reassurance. "And you're going to be an incredible mother, Adhya. I can't wait to start this new chapter with you."

Adhya's POV

The day finally arrived. I woke up with a mix of excitement and nervousness. Adi was by my side, holding my hand, his presence a source of strength and comfort.

"Are you ready?" he asked, his voice filled with love and anticipation.

I nodded, tears of joy streaming down my face. "Yes, I'm ready. Let's meet our baby."

The labor was intense, but Adi was there every step of the way, holding my hand, encouraging me, and reminding me of the incredible journey we were on together.

Finally, after what felt like an eternity, I heard the first cry of our baby. Tears of joy filled my eyes as the doctor placed our newborn in my arms.

"Welcome to the world, little one," I whispered, my heart overflowing with love.

Adishh's POV

Seeing Adhya hold our baby for the first time was the most beautiful sight I'd ever witnessed. Tears of joy streamed down my face as I looked at our tiny, perfect child.

"You're here," I whispered, gently stroking the baby's cheek. "Our miracle."

We sat there, overwhelmed with love and gratitude, knowing that our lives had changed forever. This was the beginning of a new chapter, one filled with love, laughter, and the joy of raising our child together.

In that moment, I knew that no matter what challenges lay ahead, we would face them together, as a family. And there was no greater gift than that.

Chapter 49

Adishh's POV

It's Adhya's sixth month of pregnancy, and our small get-together with both sets of parents, Advish, and Trishul was a heart-warming affair. Despite the joy and laughter, there's a lingering concern. Adhya's pregnancy has taken a toll on her health, and the doctor has strictly advised complete rest. No work, no stress—nothing that could potentially harm her or our baby.

As much as I try to stay strong, I can't hide my worry. Every time I see Adhya, I notice the fatigue etched on her face, the way she moves carefully, and how she winces with discomfort. Our parents have been incredibly supportive, always ready to help, but the truth is, I can't be with her every moment of the day.

One evening, after everyone had left, Adhya and I sat on the couch, her head resting on my shoulder. I could feel her exhaustion.

"Adi," she whispered, breaking the silence, "I think we need to talk about what the doctor said."

I sighed, gently stroking her hair. "I know, Adhya. You need to rest completely, but I'm worried about leaving you here alone when I have to be at the hospital."

She looked up at me, her eyes filled with concern and love. "Our parents suggested I go stay with them. They're neighbors, and they can take turns taking care of me. It makes sense, Adi. You won't have to worry about me all the time, and I can focus on resting."

My heart ached at the thought of being apart from her, but I knew she was right. She needed rest, and our parents could provide the support and care she needed while I continued my work. "Are you sure about this, Adhya?" I asked softly, searching her eyes for any hesitation.

She nodded, a small smile playing on her lips. "Yes, Adi. It's the best decision for our baby and me. And it's not forever. Once the baby is here and I'm stronger, we'll be back together."

I hugged her tightly, my heart heavy with emotion. "I'm going to miss you so much."

"I'll miss you too," she whispered back, tears brimming in her eyes. "But we have to do what's best for our baby."

Adhya's POV

Leaving for my parents' home was harder than I anticipated. As much as I knew it was the right thing to do, the thought of being away from Adi filled me with sadness. But the baby's health and my own had to come first.

Our parents arrived the next morning to help with the move. My mom and Adi's mom busied themselves packing my essentials, while our dads reassured Adi that everything would be fine. It was a flurry of activity, and amidst it all, I caught Adi's eyes, filled with unspoken emotion.

As the time came for me to leave, Adi held me close, not wanting to let go. "Promise me you'll take care of yourself and rest," he said, his voice thick with emotion.

"I promise," I whispered, holding him just as tightly. "You promise me you'll take care of yourself too. Don't overwork, and remember to eat properly."

He smiled, trying to be brave. "I will. And I'll call you every day. We'll get through this, Adhya."

With one last kiss, we finally let go. I got into the car, and as we drove away, I watched him standing there, looking so alone. It broke my heart, but I knew we were doing this for the right reasons.

Adishh's POV

The first night without Adhya was the hardest. The apartment felt empty and lifeless. I wandered from room to room, feeling her absence acutely. Her laughter, her presence, even the way she filled the space with warmth—all of it was missing.

I tried to distract myself with work, diving into patient rounds and paperwork, but it was futile. Every time my phone buzzed, my heart leapt, hoping it was her. And every night, I called her, needing to hear her voice to calm my restless heart.

"Hi, Adi," she greeted me warmly on our first call.

"Hey, love. How are you feeling?"

"I'm okay. Our parents are taking great care of me. I'm resting, just like the doctor ordered."

I could hear the tiredness in her voice but also the determination. "I'm glad. I miss you so much, Adhya."

"I miss you too, Adi. But remember, this is just temporary. Soon, we'll be back together, with our little one."

Her words were a comfort, but the ache of missing her never quite left. I threw myself into preparing the nursery, painting it soft, calming colors, and assembling the crib. It was my way of feeling connected to her and our baby, even when we were apart.

Adhya's POV

Being at my parents' home was both comforting and challenging. They took care of me lovingly, ensuring I got plenty of rest and nutritious food. But I missed Adi desperately. Every night, we would talk on the phone, sharing the details of our days, our hopes, and our dreams.

One evening, as I lay in bed, I felt a gentle flutter in my belly. It was the baby, moving for the first time. I laughed softly, tears of joy streaming down my face. I wished Adi could be here to share this moment with me.

When I told him about it during our call, he was ecstatic. "I wish I could have been there, Adhya. I can't wait to feel our baby move."

"I know, Adi. But soon. We'll have so many moments like this together."

As the weeks passed, I focused on staying healthy and positive. My mom would sit with me, talking about when I was a baby, sharing stories that made me laugh and cry. My dad would take me for gentle walks in the garden, reminding me to stay active in a safe way.

Adishh's POV

The weeks without Adhya were the longest of my life. I missed her with every fiber of my being. Work was a welcome distraction, but it didn't fill the void. Every night, I would sit in the nursery, imagining what it would be like to bring our baby home.

One day, as I was finishing a particularly tough surgery, my phone buzzed with a message from Adhya.

Adhya: "Hi, Adi. Guess what? The baby kicked again today, and it was so strong!"

I smiled, my heart swelling with pride and love. Me: "That's amazing, love. I can't wait to feel those kicks myself."

Finally, the day came when I could visit her. I took a few days off work, eager to see her and our baby. As I arrived at her parents' home, my heart raced with excitement and anticipation.

When I saw her, my breath caught. She was glowing, her baby bump prominent. She looked tired but happy, and I couldn't wait to hold her.

"Adi!" she exclaimed, her face lighting up as she saw me.

I rushed to her, pulling her into a gentle hug. "I missed you so much, Adhya."

"I missed you too," she said, tears of joy in her eyes.

For the next few days, we were inseparable. I cherished every moment, feeling the baby kick, talking about our future, and simply being together. It was everything I had missed and more.

Adhya's POV

Having Adi here was everything I needed. His presence filled me with strength and hope. We spent our days talking, planning for the future, and feeling the baby's movements together. It was pure joy, and I savored every second.

One evening, as we sat in the garden, Adi took my hand and looked into my eyes. "Adhya, I promise you, once the baby is here and you're feeling better, we'll be together again. We'll make our home the happiest place for our child."

I smiled, tears of happiness streaming down my face. "I know, Adi. And I promise you, I'll take care of myself and our baby. We'll be a family soon."

As the sun set, casting a golden glow over us, I felt a sense of peace and contentment. We had faced challenges and obstacles, but our love had only grown stronger. And now, as we prepared to welcome our baby into the world, I knew we were ready for whatever came our way.

Together, we could overcome anything.

Epilogue

Adishh's POV

It had been five blissful days spent with Adhya and our growing baby, who was now 7 months and 10 days old. Basking in the warmth of family and friends, I felt content. As I prepared to return to Bangalore, a bittersweet pang hit me. Leaving Adhya behind, even for a short time, was never easy, but I knew our responsibilities awaited us.

Driving along the familiar road back to Bangalore, my thoughts were consumed with memories of our time together. The laughter, the late-night talks, and the gentle caresses that spoke volumes of our deep love. It was in these moments that I felt most alive, most complete.

Suddenly, my phone rang, jolting me from my reverie. It was my mother. "Adishh," she said, her voice laced with panic, "Adhya has fallen down the steps and is unconscious. We're taking her to the hospital right now."

The words hit me like a freight train. "What? How did this happen?" I demanded, my voice trembling with fear.

"I don't know, son. She just slipped. We're doing everything we can. Get here as fast as you can," my mother urged.

Without another thought, I floored the accelerator, my car speeding down the highway. My heart raced, every minute feeling like an eternity. The thought of Adhya, our unborn child, lying vulnerable and hurt, was more than I could bear.

My heart pounded in my chest as I drove at breakneck speed towards the hospital. My mind raced with a thousand thoughts, each more terrifying than the last. I could barely see the road through the blur of my tears. "Please be okay, Adhya. Please be okay," I whispered to myself, gripping the steering wheel so tightly my knuckles turned white.

When I finally screeched to a halt outside the hospital, I didn't even bother to lock my car. I sprinted through the entrance, my breath coming in ragged gasps. "Where is she?" I demanded breathlessly at the reception.

"ICU, fourth floor," the nurse replied, recognizing the frantic look of a loved one.

I took the stairs two at a time, my legs burning with the effort. When I reached the ICU, I saw my parents and Adhya's parents standing outside, their faces etched with worry and fear.

"How is she?" I asked, my voice breaking.

"She's in there," my father said, pointing towards the ICU. "The doctors are with her now."

I felt my knees go weak. I approached the glass window, my heart clenching at the sight of Adhya lying still, hooked up to various machines. Her head was bandaged, a stark reminder of the fall she had taken.

"How could this happen?" I whispered, my voice filled with anguish. I turned to our parents, my eyes blazing with anger and hurt. "You said you would look after her! You promised!"

"Adishh, we didn't know..." my father said, his tone helpless.

I shook my head, turning away from them in disgust. I collapsed into a chair, burying my face in my hands.

My mother stepped forward, tears streaming down her face. "It was an accident, Adishh. She slipped. We tried our best to keep her safe."

"Your best wasn't good enough!" I shouted, my voice echoing down the corridor. "She's carrying our child! She needed to be safe, and you failed her!"

"We're sorry, son," my father said softly, kneeling beside me.

I took a deep, ragged breath, trying to regain my composure. "I want to see her," I said quietly.

Adhya's mother reached out, her voice breaking. "We love her too, Adishh. We would never let anything happen to her on purpose."

The weight of her words sank in, and I felt a wave of guilt wash over me. Our parents loved Adhya as much as I did. I sank to the floor, my head in my hands. "I can't lose her. I can't lose them."

My father knelt beside me, placing a comforting hand on my shoulder. "We won't lose them, son. Adhya is strong, and so is that baby. We have to believe in them."

Just then, the doctor emerged from the ICU, his expression serious. "Dr. Adishh?" he called.

I scrambled to my feet, my heart in my throat. "Yes, that's me. How is she? How's Adhya?"

"As a doctor, you can understand the current situation," he began. "She is 7 months pregnant, and there was a sudden drop in her blood pressure, causing her to faint."

Adhya's mother spoke up, her voice laced with desperation. "What does that mean for her?"

The doctor sighed, running a hand through his hair. "This is a serious case. We should go for a C-section, but the chances of positive results are quite low." He took a deep breath. "As a doctor, I will do my best."

My mother approached the doctor, her face streaked with tears. "We understand. Thank you."

As I stepped into the ICU, my heart plummeted at the sight of Adhya lying on the bed. Her face was pale, and her breathing was shallow. I approached her slowly, my eyes filling with tears. I pressed a soft kiss to her forehead, my heart breaking at the sight of her.

"I'm so sorry, Adhya," I whispered, tears streaming down my cheeks.

The doctor approached me. "Will you be part of the surgery, doctor? My suggestion is to not involve."

I nodded, feeling numb with terror and grief. Adhya was my everything, and the thought of losing her was unbearable.

I spent the next few hours in a daze, my mind filled with dark, terrifying thoughts. Finally, the doctor emerged from the OR.

"Congratulations, it's a girl baby, but..."

My world stopped. I didn't breathe, didn't move. Everything was frozen in time. I heard the doctor's words, but they seemed so far away. My heart felt like it was breaking in two. "But we can't ensure anything currently. Both mother and daughter should be under observation for a day."

I nodded numbly, unable to process what had happened. I couldn't believe it was true.

As the shock of the situation began to set in, a terrible sense of despair washed over me. I slumped into a chair, burying my face in my hands.

"She's alive," I whispered, my voice barely audible. My mother stood in front of me. "Both mother and daughter will be okay, Adi."

I glanced up, my eyes wide with terror. "No, I can't lose them," I choked, my body trembling with fear. I leaned back in the chair, my mind reeling. What was I going to do without Adhya? How could I continue without her?

"They're going to be okay, Adi," my father said softly, trying to reassure me. But I could hear the fear in his voice, see it in his eyes.

"They can't die," I cried, burying my face in my hands.

The night stretched endlessly, every minute feeling like an eternity. I sat beside Adhya's bed, my eyes fixed on her peaceful face. Our baby girl was in an incubator nearby, tiny and fragile, fighting for her life. I wanted to hold her, to love her, but I couldn't move, couldn't bring myself to leave Adhya.

She was still unconscious, and it pained me to see her that way.

I couldn't bear the thought of losing either of them. They were my world, my everything. I whispered prayers, begged for their safety, and promised to be a better husband, a better father, if only they could stay with me.

As dawn broke, I leaned back in my chair, feeling exhausted. I watched as the sun rose over the horizon, bathing the city in its light. I couldn't take my eyes off Adhya's face. My heart ached with love and fear. She looked so peaceful, her breath slow and steady, her body resting comfortably in the hospital bed.

Hours turned into days, and slowly, Adhya began to show signs of improvement. Her color returned, and her breathing steadied. The doctors were cautiously optimistic, but I couldn't relax until she opened her eyes and smiled at me.

Finally, after what felt like an eternity, Adhya stirred. Her eyes fluttered open, and she looked around in confusion. When her gaze landed on me, she smiled weakly. "Adi?"

I felt tears of relief streaming down my face as I leaned in to kiss her forehead. "I'm here, love. You're okay. Our baby girl is okay."

She looked over at the incubator, her eyes filling with tears. "She's so small."

"She's a fighter," I said, my voice choked with emotion. "Just like her mother."

We sat there in silence, holding each other, grateful for the miracle of life. Our parents joined us, tears of joy mingling with their earlier fears. We were a family, united by love and hope.

As the days passed, Adhya and our baby girl grew stronger. The doctors were amazed at their resilience, and soon, we were able to take them home. The journey had been harrowing, but it had also brought us closer, reminding us of the strength of our love and the power of hope.

Back at home, we celebrated our new beginning with our family and friends. Adhya and I looked at each other, our hearts full of gratitude and love. We had faced the darkest of times and emerged stronger, ready to embrace the future with our precious daughter by our side.

Days turned into weeks as we settled into a routine with our baby girl. The house was filled with the sweet, innocent cries of our newborn, the gentle coos and gurgles that signaled her growing strength. Adhya was still on the mend, but her spirit was unwavering. She was a warrior, just like our daughter.

One evening, as I returned from the hospital, I found Adhya in the nursery, rocking our baby to sleep. Her eyes met mine, and a soft smile played on her lips. "She's finally asleep," she whispered, her voice filled with the kind of love that only a mother could possess.

I walked over and kissed her forehead, then gazed down at our sleeping daughter. "She looks so peaceful," I said softly. "Just like you."

Adhya laughed quietly, a sound that was music to my ears. "I don't feel very peaceful. I feel like a mess most of the time."

"You're the strongest person I know," I replied, sitting down beside her. "What you've been through... what we've been through... it's incredible. You're incredible."

She reached out and took my hand, her touch warm and reassuring. "We did it together, Adi. I couldn't have done it without you."

We sat there in comfortable silence for a while, simply enjoying each other's presence. The love between us had deepened, strengthened by the trials we had faced. We were a team, ready to face whatever the future held.

As the months passed, we found a new rhythm in our lives. Adhya's health improved steadily, and our baby girl continued to thrive. Our parents, always the pillars of support, visited often, bringing with them laughter and love that filled our home.

One particular day, when our daughter was about six months old, I came home to find Adhya sitting on the floor, playing with her. The sight warmed my heart. Adhya looked up as I entered, a mischievous glint in her eye. "Guess what?" she said, her smile widening.

"What?" I asked, curious.

"Our little princess said her first word today."

I felt a surge of excitement. "What did she say?"

"She said 'Dada'," Adhya replied, her eyes sparkling with joy.

I couldn't contain my happiness. I rushed over and scooped our baby girl into my arms, showering her with kisses. "Did you really say 'Dada'?" I asked, my heart swelling with pride.

Our daughter giggled, her tiny hands reaching out to touch my face. It was a moment of pure, unadulterated joy, a memory I would cherish forever.

That night, after we put our daughter to bed, Adhya and I sat on the couch, holding each other. The challenges we had faced seemed like a distant memory, overshadowed by the happiness that filled our lives now.

"I love you, Adhya," I said, my voice filled with emotion. "You and our daughter... you're my everything."

She looked up at me, her eyes shining with love. "I love you too, Adi. More than words can say."

We kissed, a gentle, lingering kiss that spoke volumes of our love and commitment to each other. She broked our kiss and said "adi, lets plan for another kid."

With strict face "no honey, no more kids." She with sad face "why, we are enjoying our parenthood."

I with shocked face "seriously?"

She nodded with sad face "Yes, because of one incident cannot occur twice."

"But that memory will be a taruma laddu, you gone through physical but we gone through mental torture I have seen both of you with dead bed." I saw tears in her eyes.

"Okay lets not have kids." She said.

"But we can trust the process." I teased her. "What?" She raised her eyebrows.

"Means." I started kissing her neck.

"What?" She was getting flustered. "Does this mean." I was kissing her shoulders.

"What?" She asked me. Now smashed on her lips. "But i have work tomorrow." She protested.

"Then let it be late day."

She stopped protesting and let herself melt in my arms. Our kiss became deeper, our bodies coming together as one. I pulled her on top of me, enjoying the feel of her weight against mine.

She pulled back, her lips red and swollen from our kisses. Her hair was wild and disheveled, her skin flushed with excitement. She was the most beautiful sight I had ever seen, and I was mesmerized.

"Where are condoms?" I muttered, "why so punctuality towards protection sir?" She questioned, "Because last time misstake leads to my promotion to father post."

"Dont call my daughter has misstake, she our doll." She slapped me playfully.

I laughed and kissed her neck. She leaned into me, a moan escaping her lips. "Do you want more, my love?" I asked, my voice thick with desire. She nodded, her hands fumbling at my shirt. I pulled it off, throwing it to the floor. I gazed at her body for a moment, then reached for her T-shirt, tugging it over her head. Her bare breasts came into view, and I could feel myself growing hard. I kissed her neck, my hand cupping her breast. She moaned, arching into my touch.

I pulled down her pants, admiring her soft curves and smooth skin. I moved my hand lower, my fingers finding their way to her core. She was wet and ready for me, and I smiled. "You're perfect, Adhya," I whispered, pressing my lips to her neck. "And you're mine."

She gasped as I slid my cock into her, moving slowly in and out. She was so tight, so warm, and I groaned as she squeezed around me.

"Adi, faster please..." she begged, her hands gripping my shoulders tightly.

I thrust harder, pounding into her as she cried out in pleasure. "I'm close..." she moaned, her fingers digging into my skin.

I continued to move, my pace quickening as we neared the edge. She climaxed first, her body tensing with ecstasy.

"Come for me, baby," I gasped, my voice shaking with need. "Come for me, my love."

She cried out my name, her voice echoing through the room. The sound sent me over the edge, and I spilled inside her with a cry.

As I collapsed onto the bed, I held her close, not wanting to let her go. I kissed her softly on the lips, my heart filled with love and affection. "You're perfect, and i'm not yet done" I whispered.

Once again I slowly push my cock into her tight pussy.

She lets out a sharp gasp, and I freeze, worried that I might have hurt her. "Are you okay?" I ask, my tone filled with concern.

"Yes, Adi, I'm fine," she replies, giving me a reassuring smile.

I relax, leaning forward to kiss her again. She responds eagerly, her tongue tracing my lips as her hands wander over my body.

I move inside her, sliding my cock deep inside her pussy. She moans, her body quivering as I thrust again and again.

I pull back, looking down at her. She's so beautiful, and I can't help but think how lucky I am to have such an amazing partner.

I lean down, kissing her passionately as I thrust into her. She cries out in pleasure, and I continue to move, enjoying the feeling of her pussy squeezing around me.

After a while, she begins to tense up, her body tensing beneath me. "I'm close..." she whispers, her voice shaking.

"Me too," I reply, my voice hoarse with lust.

I fuck her harder, our moans mingling together in the air. Finally, she tenses up, climaxing with a cry of my name. It's enough to send me over the edge, and I come with her, filling her up with my cum.

We lie together on the bed, breathing hard and sticky with sweat. I feel satisfied and happy, but also a little sad.

After a while, I break the silence, saying "we need to get up. Go for sleep."

As I held Adhya close that night, I couldn't help but think back to the day when everything seemed so uncertain. The fear, the pain, the helplessness... it all felt like a distant nightmare now. We had come so far, and it was all because of the love we had for each other.

Watching our daughter grow, seeing the love in Adhya's eyes, made me realize just how blessed I was. Life was unpredictable, filled with ups and downs, but as long as we had each other, we could face anything.

Our journey had been anything but easy, but it had taught me the true meaning of love, sacrifice, and resilience. Adhya and our daughter were my world, and I would do anything to keep them safe and happy.

As we drifted off to sleep that night, I whispered a silent prayer of gratitude for the precious family we had created. No matter what the future held, I knew we would face it together, with love and strength.

Adhya's POV

Lying in Adi's arms, I felt a sense of peace and contentment that I had never known before. The journey had been tough, but it had also brought us closer, strengthening our bond in ways I could never have imagined.

Our daughter was a miracle, a symbol of our love and resilience. Watching her grow, seeing the world through her innocent eyes, filled my heart with a joy that words could never fully capture.

Adi's love and support had been my anchor through the toughest times. His unwavering presence, his gentle strength, had given me the courage to keep going. He was my rock, my partner, my everything.

As I closed my eyes that night, I felt a deep sense of gratitude for the life we had built together. Our love had been tested, but it had only grown stronger. With Adi by my side, I knew we could face anything that came our way.

We were a family, bound by love and hope, ready to embrace the future with open hearts. And as I drifted off to sleep, I knew that no matter what challenges lay ahead, we would face them together, hand in hand, with love as our guide.